Anticipation
and Seduction

Patrice Michelle

A SAMHAIN PUBLISHING, LTD. publication.

Samhain Publishing, Ltd.
577 Mulberry Street, Suite 1520
Macon, GA 31201
www.samhainpublishing.com

Anticipation and Seduction
Print ISBN: 978-1-59998-972-3
Anticipation Copyright © 2008 by Patrice Michelle
Susanna's Seduction Copyright © 2008 by Patrice Michelle

Editing by Linda Ingmanson
Cover by Scott Carpenter

Anticipation, 1-59998-782-1
First Samhain Publishing, Ltd. electronic publication: October 2007
Susanna's Seduction, 1-59998-596-9
First Samhain Publishing, Ltd. electronic publication: May 2007
First Samhain Publishing, Ltd. print publication: October 2008

Contents

Anticipation

What if the "one who got away"...didn't?

Deidre Nelson has never forgotten the man who stole her heart so effectively a decade ago. When circumstances bring her back to Ventura, Texas to look after her parents' B&B, she prepares to face Jonas Mendez, the sexy wrangler-turned-sheriff, with growing anticipation.

Deidre's engaging smile and seductive gaze has haunted Jonas for ten years. But life's cruel ironies pepper his past, leaving him guarded and wary. He vows to keep his interaction with Deidre strictly professional while she's in Ventura.

But when vandalism at the B&B turns life-threatening, Jonas finds himself intimately involved with the one woman he has always wanted but never touched.

As a decade of built-up anticipation becomes reality, suddenly the line between protector and possessor begins to blur.

Warning, this title contains the following: explicit sex and graphic language.

Susanna's Seduction

All it took was the right man to seduce the spontaneous woman within her...

Susan Brennon never expected that running an errand for her future sister-in-law would land her a spur-of-the-moment date. When Michael leads her down a sensual path of seduction, she takes on the sexy Italian full-throttle, all the while keeping her heart under tight guard. Every person she's formed a close attachment to has moved on. She doesn't expect Michael to be any different.

From the moment he touches Susan, Michael Piccoli wants her. But as their relationship grows more physical, he finds that for the first time in his life he desires more than sex from a woman—he wants the whole package with Susanna. Michael's determined to break through the rigid hold Susanna has on her emotions. He'll do anything to reach her, even if that means taking their relationship to a whole new level.

Warning, this title contains the following: explicit sex and graphic language.

Anticipation

Dedication

To my family, thank you for believing in me.
To my fans, thank you for your amazing support!

Acknowledgements

To my editor Linda Ingmanson, I appreciate your tenacious desire for "more".

To my critique partner Cheyenne McCray, thank you for never holding back!

Chapter One

The man I could never have, Deidre thought as the cowboy who had haunted her fantasies for a decade drove up in his blue and white police car. Her stomach muscles flexed as he cut the engine and climbed out of the driver's seat.

Her parents told her a few years back that the Flying Wind's wrangler had become the town sheriff, but nothing could have prepared her for the devastating sight of Jonas Mendez's broad shoulders decked out in a uniform, complete with a shiny silver badge. The white shirt showed off his mixed Hispanic and Caucasian skin tone to perfection, and the gun belt strapped around his black pants only added to the steely confidence he exuded, even more now than he had ten years ago.

"Miss Nelson."

When she'd agreed to watch her parents' B&B, she'd psyched herself up for this meeting. She couldn't let herself get caught up in him again. Yet, even though she knew there couldn't be anything between them, her heart sank a little that he hadn't called her Deidre. She let her smile melt away and put her hand in his warm one, shaking it with a firm grip. "Thanks for stopping by, Sheriff. My parents appreciate you making the effort."

"My pleasure, ma'am." He released her hand and touched the rim of his hat, giving her a respectful nod.

Despite his formal tone, the brief clasp of his hand around hers had ignited a burst of tingles in her arm. *Why are all the good ones always taken?* she lamented, until her brain caught up with what she'd seen, or rather what she didn't see when he'd touched his hat.

His left hand was bare.

Her heart stuttered in shock. Was there a reason he wasn't wearing his wedding band? Deidre's gaze jerked to his dark blue one in hopes he'd volunteer an answer to the question she knew reflected in her eyes.

"It's the least I can do considering I haven't been able to stop the acts of vandalism that have occurred at the Flying Wind lately," he said as he scanned the B&B and its surrounding property with an assessing gaze. "I've missed the quiet tranquility of this place."

"I heard you've taken over your parents' property now." She tried to keep her tone casual despite her pulse's rushing whoosh in her ears. "I understand the Mendez spread is pretty vast."

His jaw ticced as he squinted into the sun. "My mom died six years ago and my dad followed her a couple years later. My brother wasn't interested in running the ranch, so I took over."

Something was bothering him. His grim tone told her there was more. She tilted her head in curiosity, wanting to ask, *What's wrong? How have you been doing these past ten years? Is your favorite food still chili with lots of Tabasco? What made you decide to run for sheriff? And for god's sake why aren't you wearing your wedding ring?* "Can't be easy being both sheriff and full-time rancher."

Jonas' focus shifted to her. Fine lines were more apparent around his eyes, his bearing more intense. His shoulders might be broader, but his cheekbones were leaner, projecting a harsher, less relaxed persona than she remembered from the twenty-six-year-old wrangler she'd met a decade ago.

"I have a foreman who oversees the ranch during my office hours, but I enjoy the constant hard work."

"With very little time to relax," she finished for him before she thought better of it. *Damn, that was stupid. New York wasn't supposed to follow me.*

His mouth set in a firm line. "I prefer to stay busy."

While the late summer Texas wind whipped around them and the early evening sun dipped low in the cloudless blue sky, tense silence stretched between them. Deidre lifted her hands in the air, spreading them wide as she cast her gaze from one side of the B&B's long front porch to the other. "Well, as you can see, the Flying Wind is safe and sound, so you can head home now."

His black eyebrows drew downward. "I don't like you staying here by yourself."

He sounded so serious and forceful, she couldn't help but grin. The quiet town of Ventura, Texas was far safer than Manhattan! "Hey, no worries. I just finished my latest column for the magazine and had some free time on my hands, so I offered to housesit. My parents decided since nothing has happened at the B&B in the past three weeks, they would take their vacation before the fall season kicks into full swing. I wanted them to enjoy their first cruise without having to worry about leaving an empty house behind."

His frown only deepened.

Shaking her head at his stoic expression, she kept her tone upbeat. "I'll be fine."

He stared at her for a couple more seconds before he gave a curt nod. Reaching into his front pocket, he withdrew a business card and handed it to her. "I'll be by tomorrow around this time. Call my cell if you need me any time. My property is adjacent to your parents'. I can be here in three minutes."

And if my needs are of a more personal nature? She gave an inward sigh as she took the card. "Thanks, Sheriff."

He touched the brim of his hat once more and walked back to his car. Opening the door, he paused and leaned his arm on the window frame, regarding her with a steady gaze. "I may have more responsibilities now, but I'm still the same cowboy, Deidre. Jonas will do."

He wasn't the same laidback cowboy she remembered, but a much older, hardworking man who managed to blow through all the mental barriers she'd spent weeks building up. And all it took was seeing him with those secrets in his eyes. Her heart raced as he drove away, gravel dust clouding over the red taillights. After ten years, hearing her name again in that sexy Texan accent caused a shiver to ripple over her body. How many times had she fantasized hearing him say her name in a passionate moment? She stared at the crisp card in her hand, wishing it were six o'clock tomorrow already.

ᘓ

Ten years earlier...

Jonas' horse ambled up the wooded trail. Velvet walked behind them via the lead rope. The mare held her head low...as she should, Deidre thought with a wry smile as she turned her attention forward once more. Darn horse had scared the wits out of her, taking off like she had.

But Jonas' firm grip around her waist distracted her from her anger and made her forget about the stinging cut she'd acquired on the cheek during the skittish horse's mad dash down an unmarked trail. She glanced at his tan forearm wrapped tightly around her waist, noting the sprinkle of dark hair and the defined veins that spread up his muscles. With each step his horse took, her body dipped and swayed, molding her against Jonas' hard frame.

"I'm not gonna let you fall, darlin'." Butterflies scattered in her belly at the sensation of his fingers gripping her rib cage. His chest pressed against her back, muscular and warm. She leaned into him, inhaling his woodsy, masculine scent—a scent that had driven her nuts the last several days she'd spent at her parents' brand new bed and breakfast retreat they'd named Flying Wind. She'd thought the Texan B&B would be a nice place to visit during her fall break from college. What she didn't expect was to be instantly attracted to her parents' head wrangler in the process.

She laid her head in the crook of his neck and closed her eyes...wishing.

His warm breath came close to her temple as if he were going to say something...or kiss her. Her pulse skittered in anticipation and goose bumps formed on her skin. When he did neither, a maddening mix of relief and disappointment washed over her.

His horse slowed and she opened her eyes to see they were near the end of the wooded trail. Dusk was almost upon them and sunlight filtered through the thick trees above them, making her feel warm and secure. The smell of earth and outdoors, mixed with Jonas' heavenly scent, surrounded her in a blanket of rightness she didn't want to let go.

When he placed his hand on her thigh and squeezed, her belly tightened in instant response to the heat generated by his broad palm. She bit her lip as she lowered her gaze to his tanned hand. In a month he'd be wearing a wedding band on his ring finger. *Why didn't my parents open their business a year earlier?* she mentally wailed.

Jonas slid off his horse in one graceful, fluid movement. His black Stetson tilted until his deep blue gaze collided with hers.

As he encircled her waist to lift her down, words lodged in her throat. Once her feet touched the ground, she finally forced an appropriate response, unlike the zillion other inappropriate thoughts rumbling around in her mind. "Thank you for rescuing me."

He smiled and instead of letting her go, his grip tightened around her waist. Pulling her close, he pressed his jaw against her temple. The sensation of his chest rising and falling in a deep, shuddering breath surprised her.

"In another life..." he said in a gruff tone before he released her and moved to untie Velvet.

ᘒ

Deidre awoke with a dull ache between her legs, her heart racing. She sat up and pushed her hair away from her face, staring at the bright morning sunlight filtering past the pale green gingham curtains in the B&B's front guest bedroom. She'd lost count of how many times she'd dreamed of the last time she'd seen Jonas Mendez—the last words he'd spoken to her before she went back to college. Since then she'd had a litany of fantasies about Jonas. Of course, in *her* dream world, the sexy cowboy hadn't been engaged.

And *why* wasn't he wearing a wedding band ten years later?

Maybe he never wore one. Or his marriage had failed.

It happens.

She'd thought she was on the "right" relationship track, twice. Her last two boyfriends turned out to be work-a-holics who spent more time at the office than with her. Tom's true love was his corporate status, and Jeremy's long hours led to *playing* with a redhead in his law firm.

Irritated with herself for dwelling on Jonas' marital status and her own past miserable experiences with men, she pushed back the covers. The goats needed to be fed and her parents had asked her to fertilize the main flowerbeds while they were gone. Fortunately it had rained hard the night before and there wasn't any rain in the forecast. Now was the best time to spread the fertilizer. *Better get started on those chores. Apparently I need a distraction from fruitless ponderings.* Shaking her head, she stood and turned toward the bathroom.

ؒ

"Hey, Sheriff," the cashier called out as she swiped Deidre's credit card through the automated machine.

"Afternoon, Sally."

Deidre cast her gaze over her shoulder to see Jonas heading toward the back of the Mom-and-Pop store. His boots hit the wood floor with a heavy, purposeful stride, sending shivers down her spine. He stopped at the bottom of a ladder and spoke to the older man who was stocking extra canned goods on a top shelf.

"I'm so glad to see you back. You've grown into a beautiful lady." Deidre's attention returned to the cashier's full cheeks, which were puffed up in a broad smile.

Heat tinged Deidre's face at the compliment. "Thanks, Sally. It's great to be back. I really enjoyed my summer here while I was in college. I wish I'd come back sooner."

"Pshaw!" Sally waved her hand then bagged the last of Deidre's groceries. "You had to experience the big city rush for a while. Only then would you appreciate the relaxed lifestyle our town has to offer."

Deidre laughed and put her hands around the bag to pick it up. "Amen to that. There's a certain amount of comfort in knowing some things don't change," she commented as she glanced around the store's solid wood floor to the barrels of fresh produce on display.

"True, but there's one thing I wish would change."

Deidre elevated her eyebrow. "What's that?"

Sally's deep green gaze cut to the two men talking in the back of the store. Jonas was holding the ladder while Sally's husband climbed a rung higher to straighten some boxes. "It's about time the sheriff settled down."

The bag crumpled under Deidre's tightened fingers. "For some reason I thought he was married."

Sally exhaled an unladylike snort of disdain. "He never married." She leaned forward and spoke in a lowered voice. "Two weeks before his wedding, he caught Candice with his best friend."

Deidre's chest constricted at the news. His fiancée had cheated on him? She resisted the urge to glance back at Jonas' handsome profile.

"I'm so sorry to hear that," she heard herself saying. And she was sorry...for Jonas. Sheesh, in a small town like Ventura, everyone knew everyone's business. No wonder he appeared harder and less approachable than she remembered. Why hadn't her parents told her? Then again, they never knew about her crush on their wrangler.

She was pissed at herself, however. Sure she'd moved to New York to prove she could be successful on her own, but damn it, she'd avoided coming back to Ventura all this time. For nothing!

She'd thought about Jonas and his sexy smile often over the years, to the point she refused to come back to visit Texas. Why torture herself? Since her parents loved to travel, she'd invited them to New York for the holidays each year. They spent quality time together in her cozy apartment, and she always made sure her mom and dad had a grand time. She was glad her parents never pushed her to visit them at the B&B.

"Anyway, it's been almost ten years," Sally continued. "'Bout time he moved on, in my opinion. You married?"

Deidre couldn't help the chuckle that rumbled past her lips at the woman's direct question and surreptitious glance at Deidre's left hand. "You trying to play matchmaker, Sally?"

The older woman shrugged then smiled, an expectant look lighting her face. "So are you?"

"I'm sure my mom has shared my marital status or lack thereof with you." Deidre shook her head and grinned. "You and my mother are like two peas in a pod."

Sally let out a full-bellied laugh. "True. Dorothy and I are like long-lost sisters. I miss her company already."

Deidre's smile broadened. "She and Dad will be back in a couple more days. I'm sure they'll be full of stories of their adventures from their cruise."

Sally wagged her pudgy finger toward her. "Your mom better have taken her digital camera. I told Dot I wanted lots of photos."

Deidre started to pick up her bag of groceries when someone came from behind her and swooped the paper bag out of her arms.

"I'll carry 'em out for you, Deidre."

Jonas' serious eyes locked with hers. Without his hat shadowing his face, his eyes appeared a deeper blue than she remembered, more stormy and turbulent. No longer crew cut, his coal black hair had a wave to it that just begged to be touched. Slight changes for sure, but her pulse still raced like it had ten years ago.

"Um, thanks." She waved to Sally as she turned to walk out of the store.

"Bye, you two," Sally called out. As they walked away, Deidre caught the woman's "thumbs up" signal out of the corner of her eye.

When Jonas started to turn and say goodbye to Sally, Deidre's heart jerked. He didn't need to know they were talking about him. She grasped his elbow and tugged him out of the store. "How's your day been?"

"Sally been trying to set me up again?" The corners of his mouth turned up a little as he followed her outside.

Disappointment settled in her stomach at the amusement in his voice. This was a common occurrence, apparently. He didn't need to know it bothered her. She came to a halt next to her dark blue rental car and stuck out her bottom lip in an exaggerated pout. "And here I thought I was special."

He leaned close enough that she could smell his aftershave. God, he smelled good—spicy, musky and all male. His imposing frame blocked out the sun, dwarfing her own five-foot-nine-inch height. He might've gone through some rough times, but Jonas' charisma had magnified a hundredfold over the years. With a mere glance, he caused her body to heat in instant response.

Handing her the bag of groceries, he said in a low voice, "You've always been special," before he headed toward his police car. Once he reached the vehicle, he opened the door and called across the parking lot, "Do you still make those oatmeal chocolate chip cookies?"

She nodded. "I've tweaked the recipe a half dozen times since I graduated from culinary school."

His dark eyebrow rose. "I liked the original version. I'll stop by and check on you tonight."

When he drove past, his gaze locked with hers for a brief second, causing Deidre's skin to prickle. *I liked the original version.* The way he'd looked at her when he drove past made her wonder if he was talking about cookies with that comment.

She'd never been more aware of a man and her reaction to his presence than she was of Jonas Mendez. No man had ever come close to affecting her the way he did. From his smoldering gaze to his magnetic heat, he made her breasts ache, her stomach tighten and her breath hitch whenever he came close. Did he sense it? The crinkle of the paper bag underneath her fingers pulled her out of the seductive haze Jonas had created the moment he invaded her personal space.

After she opened her car door and set the groceries in the passenger seat, Deidre sat with a heavy sigh and acknowledged that her emotional response was part of her problem. Since she'd never been with Jonas, she wondered if she'd subconsciously built him up and put him on a pedestal, leaving the other men she'd dated lacking in many ways. Could her imagination be that cruel?

After she caught Jeremy kissing his co-worker, she'd kicked his sorry ass out. He'd begged forgiveness and said he wasn't perfect—that people make mistakes. Did she expect perfection? All she knew was she wanted the same wonderful, trusting marriage her parents had. She never planned to accept anything less for herself.

Squaring her shoulders to ward off the bitter memory, she put the key in the ignition and started her rental car with a determined twist of her wrist.

And now Jonas was a free man.

"I'll stop by tonight to check on you," he'd said.

Excitement coiled within her as she backed out of the parking space.

ଔ

Deidre smoothed her knee-length, pale yellow linen sundress then opened the front door, intending to let the summer breeze blow through the screen door as she fixed a batch of fresh oatmeal chocolate chip cookies. Of course Snowball chose that moment to squeeze past her legs and push open the screen door, bolting outside.

"Snowball!" Deidre's sandal heels clicked across the porch's wooden floorboards and down the stairs.

The cat meowed and took off toward the barn. As Deidre made her way across the pebbled lot, her shoes turned this way and that with the rocks' movement. Rock dust stirred over her bare toes, dulling the shine of her newly polished toenails. Annoyance surged, along with fear for the indoor cat's safety. "My parents will kill me if anything happens to you. Come back, you silly cat! I have to start baking."

Snowball never even looked back. Instead, his white tail disappeared through the old barn's partially opened door.

Deidre blew out an irritated breath and trekked the rest of the way to the barn with determined steps. She knew the cat was mousing.

Sliding the creaky door fully open, she peered into the barn's dim interior. "Snowball. Stop this nonsense."

As she walked inside, a light bouncing sound above her

head told her Snowball had already made his way up the wooden ladder and was in the upper loft.

She approached the ladder and stared up the length, knowing full well there was only one way he was coming back down...by being carried.

Kicking off her sandals, she put her hands on the ladder and stepped on the first rung. "Mom and Dad said they wanted to keep you forever. I'm thinking taxidermy might be a great option at the moment."

When nothing but silence greeted her, she let out a heavy sigh and began to climb.

ભ

Jonas drove up to the Flying Wind Bed and Breakfast, tense anticipation flowing through him. After he'd seen Deidre earlier, the rest of his day moved so slow he could've sworn the clock's hands moved backward at a couple points. Usually he was so lost in his work he stayed late and didn't leave until his stomach started rumbling. Today, he couldn't wait until his watch read six o'clock. Pulling to a stop in front of the B&B, he cut the engine.

Disappointment tightened his chest when he didn't see Deidre's smiling face and gorgeous long blonde hair appear in the doorway. Behind the screen door he could see the front door was open. Maybe she was in the kitchen and hadn't heard him drive up.

He opened his door and unfolded his tall frame from his car. As he walked up the steps, he wondered if he should've changed clothes first. No, that would make this trip appear premeditated. Yet only God and he knew his motivations for checking on the Nelsons' house weren't entirely altruistic. Ever since Glen and Dot Nelson told him their daughter was going to watch their home for them while they were on vacation, Deidre had invaded his thoughts.

"Deidre," he called through the screen door as he rapped on the whitewashed wooden frame.

Nothing. The tiny hairs on the back of his neck began to stand up.

So far the vandalism at the B&B had consisted of spray painted walls, some stolen equipment and a broken window. One goat had almost died. He knew goats would eat just about anything, but...

Jonas reached for the automatic weapon clipped to his hip. As he slowly pulled open the screen door, Deidre's frustrated voice reached him from a distance. He turned in that direction, tightening his fingers on the gun's grip. She sounded as if she were outside somewhere. His senses on high alert, he closed the door and listened.

Deidre called out once more, sending him running in the direction of the barn. Gravel crunched and scattered under his boots as he ate up the distance in record time, his pulse racing.

Once he entered the barn and his gaze landed on a pair of woman's sandals sitting at the bottom of the ladder, Jonas' heart skipped several beats.

"Deidre." Deep concern made his tone harsher than he'd intended.

"I'm up here."

His tight shoulders relaxed at her casual tone. He tracked her movement above him by the bits of hay dust that fell through the space between the boards. When the floorboards over his head made an eerie creak, his sense of calm evaporated once more.

"Get down from there. There's a reason your parents built a new barn. This one's not safe."

"I have to get Snowball. Be down in a sec," she called out right before he heard a heavy thump and a triumphant, "Gotcha!"

A distinct snapping sound accompanied the thick billow of hay dust from above, causing Jonas' gut to tense. When Deidre screamed, he moved with lightning speed beneath her position on the weak wood.

The floor gave way and splintered boards rained down on his head. Jonas took Deidre's full weight with her fall, catching her in his arms. Her momentum sent them both to the barn's ground floor amid broken planks and onto an old bed of hay.

Jonas got a mouthful of cat fur before Deidre scooped up the animal and stared at him in wide-eyed shock. Gripping the cat tight to her chest, she panted. Her gaze darted between the hole in the ceiling and back to him several times before she seemed to catch her bearings. "Sheesh, my stomach went straight to my throat. That was close!"

As he pushed a broken floorboard off her lap, Jonas took shallow breaths himself. He felt as if the air had been knocked clear out of his lungs, and the sensation wasn't due to having Deidre land on him. The woman had thrown him a sucker punch with one look from her gorgeous green eyes.

Her long, light brown lashes blinked several times before she regained her composure and gave him a shaky smile. "Well, I did tell you I'd be down in a second."

He chuckled at her quick wit despite the scary fall. "Yeah, darlin', but this wasn't the way I expected you to make your entrance."

"Um, thanks for rescuing me, Sheriff." She squirmed to get out of his arms and stood, her cheeks turning an endearing shade of crimson.

Jonas' body had ignited in swift awareness at their brief contact. He missed her sweet pear-blossom smell and warm softness already. As he moved to a standing position, he pulled a piece of hay from her hair. "It's Jonas, remember?"

They stared at each other. Remember? Was he asking her to remember they were on a first-name basis the last time they'd seen each other, or the unspoken attraction between them?

Her body tingled and her bra suddenly chafed her sensitive nipples. Not to mention the persistent ache that hadn't let up between her thighs since she woke this morning. What she felt for this man had quadrupled in intensity compared to her response to him in the past.

Life's experiences—the good and the bad—had a funny way of instilling steadfast certainty beyond a shadow of a doubt. She knew exactly what she did and didn't want in a man. She'd held onto that evocative memory of Jonas in the woods all these years, not just because she couldn't forget him, but because he'd made her believe there were still a few good men left in the world. "I remember." Her voice sounded breathless, husky.

He stepped closer and reached out to cup the back of her neck. Warm fingers massaged the sensitive curve of skin as his thumb traced along her jaw in a slow, seductive caress. "Do you?"

Chapter Two

His steady gaze bored into hers, analyzing, measuring her. He'd never stared at her in such a calculating way before...as if he were trying to decipher her very thoughts and motivations.

Deidre didn't speak. She couldn't. The man had her so caught up, all she could do was return his intense perusal.

He bent closer, his lips a mere half inch from hers.

She lifted her chin, anticipating, craving his kiss...desperate to know.

"I'm not the same person I was back then." He sounded almost apologetic.

"Is that person completely gone then?" Her insides melted at his nearness, his scent and the masculine virility he naturally exuded.

Heat flared in his eyes, then his expression shifted to a closed one and he took a step back as if needing to put distance between them. Before she could ask what was wrong, the cat began to squirm in her arms. Damn, how could she have forgotten about Snowball? The fall must've scared the cat into temporary passiveness.

Clamping her arms tight around the moving ball of fur, she knew the intense, seductive moment had shattered. She glanced down at the cat, seeking a diversion. "Come on, you ornery feline. Let's get you inside."

Jonas gathered her shoes and followed her out of the barn. Pebbles poked at her feet as she stepped carefully across the driveway and up the B&B stairs to the front door.

Without looking back, she wiped her dusty feet on the doormat and entered the house. As she took her time carrying Snowball down the hall and then shutting him inside her parents' bedroom, Deidre swallowed several times to calm her raging libido. She needed to get control of her emotions. No matter their attraction in the past, Jonas had pretty much just rejected her, for Pete's sake.

But it wasn't just her attraction to him that surprised her, she admitted while heading back down the hall toward the front of the house. The lump that formed in her throat at his sudden mood change concerned her. His withdrawal hurt more than it should have.

She straightened her spine, squared her shoulders and pasted on a lighthearted smile in an effort to regain control. The Jonas of her past was an ideal she'd wanted to believe in...a fantasy she'd dreamed of exploring. Nothing more. But this Jonas had turned out to have more layers than she'd expected—layers that made her want to strip them away to find the true man lurking deep inside. She had a feeling from his shuttered expression earlier, Jonas didn't want to be seen.

"Come on in," she said through the screen door before she turned and headed to the kitchen.

Jonas' boots thudded on the wood floor behind her, but she refused to turn around. Instead, she passed the long, twelve-seater table and walked through the swinging doors into the kitchen.

Pouring flour into a measuring cup, she called out in a louder voice, "Since you've stopped by to check on me, the least

I can do is offer you some fresh baked cookies." As she bent to retrieve a couple of bowls from underneath the counter, she noticed her dust-covered feet and said in a lower voice, "Then I can rinse my dirty feet."

"Then the least I can do is stay for a bit."

Jonas' amused voice sounded so close, she quickly straightened and turned in surprise.

He sat at the small café table in the kitchen, his long legs stretched out in front of him.

She hadn't expected him to follow her into her "space". Deidre set the bowls down and picked up the cooking spoon. "Only cooks are allowed in the kitchen. Unless you're helping, scoot."

"Well then..." Jonas grinned and set his hat on the table.

When he began to roll up his sleeves, Deidre stared at him. "You're helping?" *Did that really come out in a squeak?*

Jonas moved into her personal space, his broad frame making the kitchen feel very small. "You made the rules." Reaching around her, he picked up the bag of chocolate chips. "Now where's the sugar?"

Deidre rapped his hand with the spoon. "Oh, no you don't. If you're going to help, we're doing this in order."

Jonas gave her a devilish grin as he pulled open the bag of chocolate chips. "No worries, Chef Nelson. I'm just here to sample the wares," he said before popping a handful of the chips into his mouth.

Sample the wares. Was that a double entendre? Man, she couldn't tell. Taking the bag from him, she set it on the counter. "If you eat all the ingredients, we'll just have oatmeal cookies, Sher—"

Before she could finish, he stepped close and popped a

chocolate chip into her mouth. "Who can resist sampling?"

As she chewed that tiny piece of dark chocolate, the rich flavor burst in her mouth. With Jonas standing so close, dishing out sexy food phrases, the term "decadent dessert" took on a whole new meaning.

Deidre swallowed the chocolate and took a step back to clear her head. Grabbing an empty bowl, she shoved it into his hands. "Eggs. Yeah, we need air...er, eggs. Can you go collect a few from the coop?"

Jonas chuckled and turned to retrieve his hat. "Eggs. Coming right up," he said as he plunked his cowboy hat on his head and walked through the swinging doors.

The moment Jonas exited the room, Deidre poured all the dry ingredients into a bowl and set it aside. Then she quickly readied the butter and sugar in another bowl so all she had to do was drop in the eggs once Jonas returned. If she let him "help" her, her nerves would be shot. The man's presence always knocked her off-kilter. She'd be a bumbling idiot in the kitchen—the one area of her life where she'd always been very confident and successful.

As she was stirring the butter, Jonas leaned across her body to set the bowl of eggs on the counter. Her stirring hand froze and butterflies scattered in her stomach.

"What am *I* supposed to do? Looks like you're almost done," he whispered next to her ear.

I could give you plenty of ideas if you'd give me some indication, cowboy. Chill bumps formed on her arms, raising the tiny blonde hairs. She set the spoon down and grabbed a couple of eggs. Breaking them on the bowl, she tried to sound airy as she began to stir vigorously. "Have a seat. I'm almost done."

Jonas placed his hands on either side of the counter, trapping her where she stood. "Why is this the first time you've come back to Ventura?"

Deidre's pulse rushed in her ears, but she continued to stir as if he wasn't affecting every single nerve ending in her body. She paused her stirring. "My work was in New York and my parents liked the chance to travel, so I invited them there on the holidays. There's always stuff to do in the city."

He moved closer. "You didn't ever wish to get away from the city hustle and bustle to wide open spaces? You never craved these gorgeous views?"

I've craved one certain gorgeous view...too many times to count.

"I remember a young girl who loved everything 'Texas', who ran out in a fierce storm and had to be hauled back inside for her own good. If you've outgrown all that, why come back now?"

His masculine smell, combined with the sugary cookie dough aroma, turned her insides to mush.

She didn't understand why he'd walked away from her in the barn earlier, but she wasn't opening up herself for another round of hurt by telling him the whole reason she'd left. "My parents have always done everything for me, given me everything I've wanted. I knew I had a job waiting for me here if I wanted it, but I needed to prove to myself I could be successful on my own. I did well, and becoming a food critic helped fund my parents' trips to New York every year, but when they asked me to watch the B&B so they could go on vacation without worries, I saw this as something they needed *me* for. I was finally able to do something to repay them for all they've done for me, so I came back."

"Hmmm," he responded at the same time he reached into the bowl and swiped up some of the dough with his finger. "Do they teach restraint in culinary school?"

His question caught her off guard. "Why?"

"How can you resist not taking a taste?" he replied as he lifted his finger from the bowl, ready to take a bite.

Before the batter could make it to his mouth, Deidre caught his finger with her lips and sucked the cookie dough off the tip. Once she swallowed the sweet dough, she slowly slid her lips across his finger and then began stirring once more as if she hadn't just cock-teased the man. "I just need the right incentive to take a nibble."

Jonas' hand landed on her hip. His fingers gripped her firmly. "Deidre, I—"

When he stopped himself, then took the bowl out of her hands and set it on the counter, murmuring, "The cookies can wait," Deidre didn't know what to think. Yes, she'd been brazen, teasing him like that, but Jonas was sending out very confusing signals.

Deidre let him lead her to the straight-back chair next to the table. When he sat her down and turned to fill an empty bowl with water, she just stared in confusion.

She was surprised when he lowered himself to one knee and put the bowl of water on the floor next to her feet. Her pensive gaze tracked his sexy, hard-working hands as he withdrew a white handkerchief from his pants pocket and dipped the cloth in the water, his movements measured and precise.

The tense silence between them was killing her. "What are you doing?"

Instead of replying, his warm fingers wrapped around her left ankle and his gaze locked with hers, steady and sure.

Totally perplexed, she let him lift her foot above the bowl. When he glanced at her foot and began to wipe the warm wet cloth along her skin, bathing away the gravel dust, a lump clogged her throat at the personal, almost reverent act.

Tears formed as her emotions rushed to the surface once more. Blinking back the wetness, she swallowed hard and tried to keep her voice from shaking. "In the barn, you backed away from me. I don't understand."

"Let it be, Deidre."

His voice was harsh, cold...almost angry, but his touch told a different story. While one hand gently bathed away the dirt, the other massaged her calf in a seductive caress, as if he couldn't stop himself from touching her.

The man baffled her. She knew about his past...a past that she was certain caused a lot of hurt, but she'd endured her share of failures in relationships, too. If he didn't want to talk, but instead wanted his hands to speak for him, then so be it. For now.

When he began to work on her other foot, her gaze scanned his crisp white shirt stretched across his broad shoulders. She acknowledged how much his sheriff's shirt and black pants, combined with the sight of his gun strapped to his hip, turned her on. Yet there was one thing she'd wanted to do since she'd seen him yesterday. Pulling off his cowboy hat, she tossed it on the table.

He paused for a second, but he didn't look up as he resumed his ministrations. Her heart swelled when his hands began to massage the curve of her calf. From the top of his black-as-sin hair to the tips of his cowboy boots, he might be a sheriff now, but he was still her cowboy. Goose bumps formed on her skin as her gaze focused on his short, dark hair. Thoughts of running her fingers through the thick, slightly wavy mass flashed through her mind.

He moved the bowl out of the way and his hands slid upward, pushing her skirt past her knees. When he spread his palms across the outside of her thighs, Deidre's breath hitched.

She gave in to the urge and ran her hands through his hair, enjoying the thick silk bending around her fingers.

At her touch, Jonas' fingers gripped her skin in a possessive hold. His warm breath bathed her inner thighs as he ran his hands up her hips to grip her buttocks. The moist sensation of his warm breathing brushing the top of her thighs, so close yet so distant, only made her body pound for more.

Jonas set his other knee on the floor and finally spoke, his voice gravely and low. "Let me cherish you the best way I can."

The torture and anguish in his tone burrowed deep in her heart, unlocking more than a physical response...so much more. Deidre bit back the swift desire to wish for more from him. No matter how strongly she felt for him, his words told her he wasn't capable of giving on an emotional level.

In answer, she relaxed her thighs and gripped his shoulders. Gathering him close, she kissed the top of his head.

Tension eased from his shoulders at the same time he slid her short skirt even higher. The glide of the soft material against her skin, flanked by the heat from his palms, sent tiny tremors skittering through her body. Silence echoed around them, punctuated by an occasional faint *naaaa* of the goats through the open kitchen window.

Jonas bent to place a tender kiss on her inner thigh and Deidre's pulse stuttered at the surreal moment. No amount of fantasizing had ever come close to the barrage of sensations his real-life actions elicited within her. Her heart thumped and her belly tensed with skittish butterflies. Heat radiated from that one kiss and her skin tingled when the next one, wetter, hotter and more tender than the last, moved higher.

Her tense muscles began to relax, like a bowl of butter heated to its melting point. An unbidden moan rushed past her lips, so very primal it surprised her.

"Jonas," she murmured.

His mouth moved higher and he nipped at the curve where her inner thigh met her body. "Say it again, darlin', just like that. The need in your voice...damn, it makes me throb."

His fingers gripped her buttocks harder and he pulled her body forward, placing an open-mouthed kiss over her cloth-covered sex.

Deidre jerked at the deeply intimate act, keening in ecstasy. The sensation of his hot, moist mouth sending heat through her underwear was the sexiest turn on she'd ever experienced. Her heart jack-hammered hard against her chest, making her pant to keep up with its erratic pace.

"I want to hear it, Deidre." He ran his teeth across her clit then let out a low moan of his own before he nipped at the fleshy top of her mound.

His love bite sent an erotic shudder of excitement jolting through her. Her fingers twisted in his hair and her head fell back against the chair as she called his name in an intense cry of need.

In answer, he ran his tongue along the underwear, softly at first and then more insistently. Finally he thrust against the thin material, slightly penetrating her entrance.

"Even through your panties your taste is driving me nuts," he rumbled. His tongue traced the side of the soft material, flicking at the elastic edges, seeking entrance.

Deidre's heavy breathing increased and her thigh muscles tensed once more. Her hips began to rock of their own accord. She wanted to tell him to tear the damn scrap of cloth off, yet her emotions warred. Something about the man using only his tongue to push the barrier away was incredibly primal, sending her libido into hyperdrive.

She waited, her body a taut bowstring. His tongue swiped

35

past the barrier and along the moist edges of her sex, his groan reverberating against her soft folds.

Her nails dug into his scalp and her hips naturally canted toward him, her body frantic for his mouth to make contact. So close...so very close.

A loud intercom squawk caused her to jerk in surprise right before a disembodied voice said, "Sheriff Mendez, I know you just got off, but we need you down at the station ASAP!"

When Jonas raised his head and the pissed expression on his face changed to an apologetic one, she wanted to scream, "Hell no! You're not going anywhere!"

Frustrated disappointment surged through Deidre, making her stomach ache, but if she didn't make light of the situation, she'd cry. "Tell him you haven't gotten off yet, but when you're done, you'll get right back to him."

Jonas' blue eyes crinkled with laughter. He gave her sex a hard kiss before he straightened and moved to his feet. "I'm sorry, but I need to respond," he said as he grabbed his cell phone from his hip.

While he said into his phone's walkie-talkie, "Be there in five, Jeff," Deidre pushed her skirt down and stood beside him.

As he slid the cell phone back in its clip, she realized with shock that she'd almost let the man give her oral sex and she'd yet to kiss him. How had they managed to completely skip all the foreplay? She placed a shaky hand against her mouth, stunned at her wanton behavior. *God, he must be exuding some kind of pheromone or something! That has to be why I'm acting like this.*

Lowering her hand, she straightened her shoulders and composed her expression to what she hoped passed as a nonchalant, worldly one. "Well, I know you have to go—"

Before she could finish, Jonas lifted her chin.

Her heart melted under his penetrating gaze.

Cupping the back of her neck, he pulled her against his chest. His blue gaze, serious once more, searched hers before his line of sight dropped briefly to her lips.

His thumb brushed across the soft skin, the work-roughened texture making her knees wobble. "Never doubt it. I'm looking forward to exploring every part of your body in excruciating detail."

The heated look coupled with his sexy tone completely dissipated her apprehension. "How did you know what I was thinking?"

"Because you have some of the most expressive eyes I've ever seen, sweetheart."

She let out a self-depreciative laugh. "Great, I guess I know why I'm never successful with April Fools pranks."

Smiling, he kissed her on the forehead. "I have no idea how long I'll be. Can I stop by later?"

Deidre wrapped her arms around his waist and laid her head on his shoulder for a brief second. She inhaled his heady masculine scent until her lungs couldn't hold any more air. His hard, well-built body made her ache all over again. With a heavy internal sigh, she nodded her assent.

Jonas folded his muscular arms around her waist and hugged her tight. He placed a quick kiss on her hair before he released her and started to walk through the swinging kitchen doors. He paused and his gaze returned to hers, laser sharp.

"Don't plan on getting any sleep tonight. We've got ten years of anticipation built up, darlin', and I sure as hell plan to make every moment count."

CR

As Jonas walked away from Deidre, his gut tightened. Sure he had a hard-on from hell, but the coiled tension inside his belly made him feel lightheaded, like a teenager on his first hormonal high. This woman with her sexy smile and sultry gaze had him wound up so tight—hell she'd done so ever since he'd laid eyes on her.

When Deidre said she came back to help her parents and didn't act as if she'd thought about him at all, he wasn't sure what, if anything, still lingered between them. Which was probably for the best, considering he'd vowed to keep their relationship professional while she was in Ventura.

Then she went and wrapped her lips around his finger, sucking hard, and he was done. There was no doubt that what had lingered between them a decade ago, that magnetic, white-hot attraction, was still there, waiting for the first match to be struck.

Once he touched her in the kitchen, he couldn't stop, and her avid encouragement only fueled his libido. Deidre seemed to know he'd give what he could, but touching her like he wanted after all these years...he could get so caught up in her.

He shook his head to clear it, tamping down the raw emotions raging in his gut.

Candice had ruined him...had taken away his belief in eternal love and the sanctity of promises made.

Despite his physical attraction to Deidre when he'd met her over ten years ago, he'd suppressed his reactions. He'd been on the verge of marrying a good woman...or so he'd thought. Little did he know Candice had been cheating on him since even before their engagement.

Had he subconsciously known about Candice's deceitful nature all along but refused to believe it? he wondered as he got in his car and drove away. Seeing Deidre again made him question the past—to look at it with a different pair of eyes—a past he'd refused to examine under the microscope. Until he came face to face with a pair of familiar dewy green eyes that had jerked at his soul and haunted his dreams for a decade.

Setting his jaw, he gripped the steering wheel tight. Despite his powerful feelings toward Deidre, he refused to allow himself to trust another's or his own judgment when it came to relationships. He was glad Candice and Jake had left town right after they got married so he wouldn't be constantly reminded that one failed engagement peppered his past and hurt him deeply. He should count himself lucky he never got to the point of saying, "I do". As far as he was concerned, he would never utter those two words.

Chapter Three

Deidre twisted her hair up and away from her face for the fifteenth time then finally let it fall in frustration. With just a bit of wave, her blonde locks never had the softness of perfectly straight hair or the lively bounce of curly hair. Instead it always looked as if she'd finger-combed it to death. She finally gave up and focused on her outfit. After the fall in the barn had stained her yellow dress, she'd changed clothes, picking out a soft cotton, spaghetti-strapped tank top in a sea foam green and a white crushed cotton skirt.

A commanding, heavy knock at the front door reverberated all the way down the hall and into the guest bedroom, making her heart skip several beats. Her skirt swirled around her ankles as she turned and left the bedroom, excitement causing goose bumps to form on her skin.

Biting her lip, she glanced at her watch. An hour and a half had passed since Jonas had gone back to the office. The last remnants of the day's sunlight shined on the hall's oak flooring as she made her way to the front door.

When she opened the door, her stomach dipped and spun at the mouth-watering sight before her. Jonas' old weathered brown Stetson was pulled low over his brow. He propped his forearm on the doorframe, his intense blue gaze staring down at her, while she took in every mouth-watering detail. His heather gray T-shirt and worn jeans fit his muscular frame, and a wide silver belt buckle and scruffy brown boots rounded out his devastating, born-'n-bred cowboy look.

Dear God, he looked every bit the man who'd stolen her heart and ruined her for all men so long ago. His uniform might've turned her on, but seeing him like this again made her entire body quake.

"Evenin', Deidre. The house smells like fresh-baked cookies." His respectful nod, combined with the seductive sweep of his gaze up and down her body in an openly frank appraisal, had an overwhelming effect she hadn't thought possible. Her knees actually gave way.

Grabbing the doorknob to keep from making a complete fool of herself, Deidre ground her teeth at the rush of embarrassed heat that crept up her cheeks. "I...um, didn't hear you drive up."

"You okay?"

At the concern in his tone, she straightened and released the doorknob with a quick nod. "Never better. Would you like a cookie?" *How dull was that? Damn, I need to sign up for conversation lessons.*

He shook his head slowly. "Maybe later." A wide grin spread across his face as he turned to let her see his horse tied to the porch behind him. "You didn't hear me drive up, because I brought a quieter ride. Remember Admiral?"

Admiral snorted while nodding his head.

Deidre glanced at Admiral and her lips tilted in amusement as she spoke to the horse. "I'm much more confident riding now than I was back then."

"I'm sure you are," Jonas said, drawing her attention. His jaw flexed and desire flashed in his deep blue eyes as he held his hand out to her. "Come ride with me."

She didn't miss the edge in his lowered tone, and something about the possessive look in his eyes both surprised and thrilled her. How many times had she wished to see him gaze at her just like that? She ran her palm across her skirt and took a step back. "Let me go change first."

Jonas reached out and grasped her hand, bringing her fingers to his mouth. "You're perfect just as you are." When he pressed his warm lips against her skin, his stare enticing and persuasive, she lost all ability to banter. Or was it his kiss that sent a tingling sensation sliding down her arm and shooting straight to her nipples?

"I...um...I'll lock up the house."

His low chuckle seemed to follow her as she turned and headed for the kitchen to retrieve the house key off the counter.

Once she'd locked the door and walked down the stairs to stand beside Jonas, the air around them grew strangely quiet. He slid his hands around her waist. She relished every second of his warm palms touching the bit of skin below her tank top as he easily lifted her up on his horse.

Deidre tried to sit sidesaddle, but Jonas squeezed her waist. "You'll have to sit astride, darlin', or it'll make for an uncomfortable ride."

She squirmed nervously at the idea of sitting astride in a skirt. "I really should go change clothes—"

Before she could finish, he gripped her hip with one hand and slid his other hand up her calf, pushing her skirt up until her thigh was bared. "Lift your leg over."

At his soft command, she did as he asked and moved her right leg over the horse's back. Without a word, Jonas swept up on the saddle behind her.

"Comfortable?" She tilted her eyebrow, casting a quick gaze over her shoulder.

"Not quite," he whispered in her ear. At the same time, he used his thighs and hips to slide her body forward until her bunched skirt was all that sat between her pubic bone and the saddle horn.

Molding his chest to her back and his thighs around her hips, he put his arms around her waist and unwound the reins from the top of the saddle horn. "Now I'm ready."

The sensation of the hard horn between her thighs and the cowboy's muscular body surrounding hers sent her heart rate soaring. Deidre gripped the top of the horn and let out an edgy laugh. "Just don't gallop, 'kay?"

Jonas urged the horse into a walk toward the trails behind the B&B. "We'll take it nice and slow, I promise."

As they entered the darkened woods, Deidre shivered at the change in temperature. Even though the evening sun slanted through the canopy of trees, bathing her skin in ribbons of diluted golden warmth, the forest's shade brought an exciting coolness in contrast to Jonas' body heat radiating against her back. She closed her eyes, enjoying the sensual combination.

"Does this trail lead to the Mendez property?" she asked.

"Mmm, hmm." His chest rumbled against her back as he rubbed his nose along her neck. "Do you want to know how many times I've thought about you?"

She jerked her eyes open, surprised by his question. "How many?"

His left hand spread across her exposed thigh and his fingers tightened around the bare flesh. "I've lost count."

Jonas' sincere admission caused the butterflies in her stomach to stir in haphazard abandon. Earlier today might have been about emotional limitations, but tonight was about confessions, she realized. "I've never forgotten you."

He gripped her thigh harder. "I never cheated on her."

Deidre understood the anguish in his voice. She placed her hand over his, her heart tripping at a rabbit's pace. "I know. Your integrity was one of the things I admired so much about you."

His body tensed behind her. "I'll never say the words 'will you marry me' again."

The vehemence in his words told her just how much his ex-fiancée's betrayal had hurt him. Deidre's heart went out to this strong, self-contained man. Even though his statement tore her up inside, she admired him more for being honest with her upfront.

Running her hand across his warm one, she laced their fingers together and let out a soft sigh. "We've both had our share of disappointments in life. I just want to feel your arms around me. I don't have any expectations beyond that."

Jonas brushed her hair to the side and buried his nose against her neck. "I'm sorry, Deidre. You blew me away the moment I saw you again after all these years. There needs to be pure honesty between us."

"No expectations, Jonas....just anticipation," she said at the same time the tiny niggling voice in her mind dared to rear its ugly head. *I hope I haven't built you up in my mind to be a bigger-than-life, beyond exceptional lover.* But the throbbing ache between her legs reminded her that the man definitely knew how to leave her wanting.

"Anticipation," he said in a husky tone as he laid the reins across Admiral's neck. The horse continued to plod along without guidance as if he knew the trail well.

Deidre's pulse thrummed when he placed his hands on her legs then slid her skirt higher, exposing her thighs completely.

He cupped his fingers along the bend of her legs and began

circling his thumbs on her muscles just above her knees. She bit her lip to keep from moaning when sensation after sensation rocked through her.

As he moved his hands higher, massaging her muscles in small circles, tiny tremors started in her inner thighs and slowly wound their way to her sex. With a low growl rumbling in his chest, Jonas shifted his weight forward in the saddle, forcing her body fully flush against the saddle horn until she literally rode the hard surface.

Each dip and sway of the horse's movements caused her mound to rub and bump against the saddle horn. Agonizing friction built and ricocheted through her sex, tensing her lower muscles. Deidre tightened her thighs around the horse and swallowed a moan.

"I feel your tension. I know you're holding back. I want to hear your excitement," Jonas said at the same time he gripped her inner thighs and forced her legs open wider. His action no longer allowed her to stop the constant pressure against her sensitive parts. Deidre began to pant then gasp each time the horse's movements made her body meet the molded surface.

Jonas moved his thighs behind hers, keeping her sex flush with the horn. The sensation of his hard cock pressing against her backside made her want to whimper.

"Your sweet ass rubbing against me is a helluva cock-tease," Jonas said in a husky tone. His hands slid up her rib cage until they covered her breasts. "Do you feel how much I want you?"

As his fingers brushed across her hard nipples, exquisite pleasure shot through her breasts and down her center. Deidre let her head fall back on his shoulder, shutting her eyes tight. The heat radiating from his hard erection seeped right through their clothes. She'd never been more stimulated.

"Yes, and it's definitely mutual," she managed to babble out while a multitude of arousing sensations battled within her. The horse had slowed, but each step became a sensual punctuation to the built-up emotions roiling inside her. Her panting turned rampant as her sex began to throb, ready for release. "Jonas... I'm..."

"I know, sweetheart. Let go. I want to hear your scream," he said at the same time he slid his fingers forward and pinched her nipples hard.

Deidre barely registered his warm breath on her neck and his tender kiss grazing the sensitive spot below her ear. Her body took over and she cried out, arching her back. Sexual tension had built to a fevered pitch within her, refusing to back down.

Jonas' sexy growl preceded an aggressive thrust of his hips, which forced her to grind incessantly against the horn. Her breath hitched in eager response to his dominant action. Deidre knew his lovemaking would be this raw and primal, and just as exhilarating. Unable to move back, she rode against the hard surface, seeking release from the coiled arousal spiking within her.

Her body tensed and her heart seemed to skip several beats right before her climax spiraled within her. With one hand on the saddle horn, she gripped the back of Jonas' neck and turned slightly, burying her face against his throat and jaw as the waves of her orgasm began. Body-rocking, heart-stopping splinters of pleasure rolled through her. Her thighs clenched the horse's sides and she drank in Jonas' sexy masculine smell while reveling in each sensual quiver that flowed through her body.

Once her heart rate began to slow, Jonas cupped her breasts and pulled her back against his chest. "Damn, woman.

That has to be one of the most erotic experiences..." His voice broke and he laid his forehead on her shoulder, exhaling a shuddering breath.

Now that her senses were returning, Deidre realized the horse had stopped walking. Jonas was breathing hard...harder than she was at the moment.

She glanced around her and noted they'd stopped at the very same spot Jonas had lifted her down from his horse ten years before—the same day he'd said, "In another life..."

When he lifted his head, she kissed him on the jaw and smiled. "Does this place look familiar?"

"We're on Mendez property now," he said in a tight voice before he lowered himself from the horse.

"I never knew that." Deidre didn't know what to think about the brief change in his mood when he lifted her down without a word. Once her feet touched the ground, she laid a hand on his chest, her stomach tightening in worry. "Jonas?"

His hands moved to her shoulders and then to the back of her neck, massaging the muscles. He pulled her close and his lips hovered over hers. Deidre's heart began to hammer all over again.

"Now I can finally do something I've wanted for a decade," he murmured.

The banked tension in his shoulders conveyed just how much restraint he employed. Jonas' fingers trembled ever so slightly as he slid them into her hair. Cupping the back of her head in a firm hold, he covered her lips with his.

As his mouth slanted across hers and the dominant thrust of his tongue demanded the same instant response, Deidre fell deeper into his strong embrace. Every warm, wet nuance of their tongues' seductive slide against each other, their bodies melding into one another while their hearts thumped in tandem

47

staccato beats, sent a heated flush of thrilling erotic vibrations all the way to her toes.

Jonas' kiss was so thorough and mind-numbingly sexy as hell. He blew through her expectations—he was decadent, chocolate sin. She relished every rasping movement of his mouth over hers, craving more.

She wrapped her arms around his trim waist and kissed him back with just as much fervor. From his shoulders' bunched muscles, to his tight grip on her, to the hard press of his mouth against hers, his kiss had a possessive undertone, as if he feared she might bolt any second. Deidre wasn't going anywhere. The man fulfilled every fantasy she'd ever had about him, ten times over. And all this before he ever slid inside her.

He lifted his head and his breathing came in heavy pants as he leaned over her shoulder to pull something from his horse's saddle bag.

Jonas' intense expression sent a shiver down her spine as he released her and held out a jean jacket. He seemed to be waiting for her to put it on. Deidre raised an eyebrow, but slipped her arms inside the material without question.

As soon as she'd pulled on the jacket, Jonas lifted her in his arms and carried her off the path to set her feet on the ground in front of a tree.

When he placed his hands on her shoulders, she felt them tremble slightly as he stared into her eyes. "I've never ached for a woman as much as I have for you."

Without even trying, this man stole her heart. He swept it right out of her chest and thrust it back, beating so rapidly she didn't know if her breathing could keep up with its thunderous pace.

Despite her best efforts to remain unemotional, tears welled. "Kiss me, cowbo—"

Jonas didn't give her a chance to finish. He yanked her hard against his chest and his lips claimed hers once more.

Deidre expected a frantic, hard kiss. Instead, the tender brush of his lips across hers only seduced her further. He suckled her bottom lip before his tongue slid inside her mouth to glide alongside hers in a leisurely, yet decadent, sensual dance. Moist heat flooded her core with each slow swipe.

Deidre responded in kind. Her hands skimmed his chest then continued upward until her fingers speared through his hair. When she knocked his hat off and began to suck on his tongue, Jonas let out a primal grunt, cinching his hands around her waist. His kiss deepened, moving more possessively across hers as he lifted her and set her back against the huge oak tree behind them.

The rough, unyielding surface of the bark behind her, coupled with the hard muscles flexing underneath her fingers, made Deidre's skin prickle in fervent response.

Jonas' fingers slid her skirt up, lifting it until his warm hands connected with her thighs. "Your skin is so soft," he mumbled against her mouth, then he kissed her jaw as his fingers traced a seductive path up her inner thighs toward her sex.

A sexy smile tugged his mouth upward as his fingers touched a patch of moisture along the inside of her leg. "The fact you're so wet makes me want you even more."

Deidre's sandals crunched the dead leaves under her feet as she spread her legs wider. She licked her lips and let her eyes close slightly. "Touch me. I've waited long enough."

"My pleasure, darlin'," he said, and cupped her sex with an aggressiveness that almost sent her over the edge.

The surprised look that crossed his face when he realized she didn't have any underwear on made her smile. "Thought I'd make it easy for you."

"The better to have you whenever and wherever I want," he rasped as he stepped closer, towering over her. His expression turned impossibly sinful right before he thrust a finger deep inside her. Deidre let out a gasp at the pleasurable invasion.

When he circled his finger, touching all the right places deep inside her, then rubbed the pad on her G-spot, she gripped his shoulders. His actions caused carnal sensations to quickly build inside her.

"You make me burn, Dee. I want you so damn bad I might lose it just unbuttoning my pants."

No, she mentally screamed. Gripping his belt buckle, she yanked it open. "We certainly can't have that," she replied as she pulled on his jeans button and unzipped his pants for him.

When her fingers brushed against his erection through his fitted gray cotton briefs, Jonas shuddered. He quickly withdrew his finger from her body to grip her wrist and pull her hand away. "Darlin', I'm so primed right now, a breeze would send me over."

She chuckled at his comment while she continued to tug on his jeans and underwear until they were past his knees.

When her gaze landed on his heavily veined erection, jutting full and proud against his lower abs, she whispered, "I want to touch you," as she dug her nails into her palm to keep from doing exactly that.

Heat flared in Jonas' gaze before he closed his eyes and laid his head back, facing the darkening sky. "Then touch me, sweetheart."

Chapter Four

Deidre's heart hammered as she uncurled her fingers and surrounded his hard erection with her hand. His skin felt so silky soft she couldn't resist sliding her hand down his impressive length to the base.

"Fuck!" he barked at the sky through clenched teeth.

She noted his hands were clenched by his sides and glanced up to see the tendons on his neck standing out as if he were exerting tremendous effort not to react to her touch.

Bending over, she gave the tip of his cock a tender kiss then straightened. "My thoughts exactly."

Jonas' blue gaze lasered into hers at the same time his hands gripped her thighs. "Condom." The word came out on a low groan.

"Which pocket?" she asked as she bent and tugged at his jeans waistband.

"My right. Front."

Deidre fished around in his front pocket and grabbed the packet. Without a word, she ripped open the plastic and began to slide the protection down his engorged erection.

Jonas' hips flexed forward and his eyes closed. With each brush of her fingers along his cock, he let out harsh breaths until she'd placed the condom completely over him.

Once she'd finished, his breathing had turned shallow. With her hands on his shoulders, Jonas gripped the back of her thighs and effortlessly lifted her up until the tip of his cock rested against her entrance. The sensation of his erection barely touching her felt so erotic she squeezed her pelvic muscles to stop the achy sensation pulsing within her. God, she'd never been more ready in her life.

Jonas held her suspended above him, his cock brushing her entrance for a couple of long heart-stopping seconds. A sudden look of sheer unadulterated lust crossed his face and his fingers tightened around her thighs. "I feel how hot and wet you are through the condom."

She wound her fingers in his hair and gave the thick locks a slight yank. "Ten years is a long time to yearn."

His arms began to quake and a look of primal possession flashed in his eyes as he took the couple steps toward the tree. Setting her back against the surface, he gripped her backside and thrust deep inside her.

She wanted to scream in fulfillment. He felt *that* good.

A shudder shook his frame and he murmured her name at the same time he withdrew and pistoned back inside her channel so hard her back slid up the tree trunk several inches.

The slick slide of his cock rubbing against her walls made a jolt of animal-like need take over her body. In the span of two heart beats, she realized exactly why Jonas made her wear his denim jacket. He was protecting her skin from the tree's rough bark. Her respect for his thoughtfulness deepened as she dug her fingers into his shoulder muscles.

Tightening her thighs around his waist, Deidre pulled her body flush with his then ran her tongue along his neck. She nipped at his skin, satisfied at the groan that pushed past his lips. "Sex with you is exactly how I thought it would be. You're rough yet tender in the ways that matter. I want more," she demanded in a heavy whisper next to his ear.

Jonas' breath escaped in a deep bellow as his fingers massaged her rear. "Deeeeidre," he said before he pressed her body against the tree and leaned into her, thrusting upward. Seated deep inside her, his entire body primed and tense, he buried his nose against her neck, and said in a ragged voice, "I want to take you so deep and hard it scares me."

The slight tremble in his low-spoken words made her heart trip several beats. She placed her hands on his cheeks and lifted his head so he had to look at her. "It should only scare you if I didn't want it." Her heart pounded and small pre-climactic tremors started in her sex as she clenched her inner muscles around his cock. "I definitely want it. I want every bone-crushing, body-rocking, ram-until-I-scream thrust. Give me the fantasy I've masturbated to on more nights than I care to remember. I want the ride of my life and I know you're the man to give it to me."

Her last words caught in her throat as he began to grind his hips against hers in slow, measured circles. "The idea of you masturbating while thinking of me is the hottest turn on."

The heavy press of his body against her clit felt so good. With each slow circle he made, her breath hitched a little higher. "Yes," she breathed out as she closed her eyes and hammered her fist against his shoulder. Her stomach muscles clenched while almost-there vibrations feathered her core in teasing pulses.

"Open your eyes," he demanded at the same time he rolled his hips against her pubic bone, this time in the opposite direction. "I want you to see the man who's deep inside you. I'm no dream man, Deidre. I'm flesh and blood and so damned jacked-up by your arousing body I can't think straight."

Her gaze locked with his intense one and she slid her hand into his shirt collar. She brushed her fingers teasingly against his skin before digging her nails into the warm flesh on his shoulder. "That makes two of us. Make me come, cowboy."

As soon as she spoke, Jonas quickly withdrew and slammed into her once, twice, a third time. He was on his fourth thrust when her body clenched tight and her orgasm crashed through her. "So...so good," she stammered, her walls tightening and releasing in euphoric spasms. With every shuddering contraction within her core, her pulse soared higher while her nipples throbbed from the erotic friction of his chest rubbing against hers.

Jonas stopped his thrusts, burying himself inside her while she gyrated her hips and rode his erection through the rest of her climax.

When she came down from her high, the look of sheer willpower on his face, the hard, on-the-edge tension made her want to cry. "Aren't you going to—" she started to ask.

"Had no idea how damned sweet you'd be," he said softly as he withdrew and sank back inside her channel, his movements a slow, methodical, determined rhythm.

When her body began to respond to his pace, her nipples tightening and her juices gathering once more, Deidre leaned close and whispered in his ear, "Come for me, lover."

And that was all it took. Jonas let out a low growl as his tempo quadrupled in speed. Fast and furious felt just as glorious to Deidre, but apparently the man refused to go over the edge alone.

"I want you to scream."

"I'm fine. Let go," she panted.

"To hell with that," he said through clenched teeth at the same time his fingers moved closer around her rear and pulled her butt cheeks apart.

The sensation of his fingers separating and stretching her sensitive skin was a surprising turn on. Deidre gripped his shoulders and tensed her body, keening as her walls shuddered with an even more explosive, higher-pitched orgasm.

"That's it, sweet Dee," he grunted out, satisfaction lacing his tone. His shoulder muscles flexed under her fingers and his hips moved faster and faster until he let out an animalistic groan as his own climax rushed through him.

When Jonas' orgasm ended and he leaned against her, breathing heavily, Deidre welcomed his weight. Wrapping her arms around his neck, she held him close. The sensation of his heart beating at a thunderous pace against her chest while he was still buried deep inside her evoked a peaceful sense of rightness within her.

She knew she didn't have a right to feel this way. Jonas had been perfectly upfront and honest with her as to the limit of his involvement. Physically he was all there. Emotionally she'd have to look elsewhere.

Soon enough she'd have to come back down to earth, but as she kissed his jaw and breathed in his outdoorsy, all male scent, she told herself she'd bask in the brief moment of idyllic perfection for as long as he'd let her.

Or until the smell of smoke captured her attention.

Lifting her nose toward the sky, she sniffed again, deeper this time. "Do you smell that?"

Jonas withdrew from her then set her down on the ground as he inhaled deeply. Backing up a few feet, he stared past the forest's tree line. His gaze jerked back to hers, a frown creasing his brow. "The smoke is coming from the direction of the B&B."

"Holy shit!" Deidre quickly pushed her skirt down. As she climbed up on Admiral, Jonas disposed of the condom and zipped up, buckling his jeans in record time. Once he retrieved his hat, he pulled himself up in the saddle behind Deidre. Wrapping his arms around her waist, he said in a serious tone, "You okay with galloping back?"

In response, she kicked her heels into the horse's side, impatient to get back to her parents' house as fast as the horse would take them.

Jonas gripped her tight against his frame and together they moved as one with the horse's fast gait. They reached the B&B in time to see black smoke billowing out of the old barn. As horrified as Deidre was by the sight, what frightened her most was a thin path of burning flames in the grass that led straight to the house. Her heart jerked when she saw the wood stairs were already on fire.

She pointed toward the house, her voice a few octaves higher. "The stairs—"

"I see them," Jonas said in a calm tone as he stopped his horse. He handed her his cell phone. "Press two to call the station. Tell Jeff I want him here now. He'll call the fire department for you."

Before she could utter a word, he was stomping out grass that was still burning near the stairs before he headed toward the back of the house.

Deidre's hands shook as she dialed the sheriff's office. When Jeff answered, she barely remembered her conversation with him because she was so intent on Jonas' disappearance. Where had he gone?

When he came around the side of the house carrying the garden hose with him, she let out a sigh of relief.

Jonas called to her to move farther away from the burning barn as he started spraying down the stairs.

Adjusting herself better in the saddle, Deidre grabbed

Admiral's reins and directed the horse to a safer spot. Once she got down, she tied his reins to the wooden fence surrounding the new barn on the other side of the B&B then ran back over to Jonas' side.

He'd managed to put out the fire on the porch, but fear and panic for her parents' home and livelihood caused her heart to thump and her legs to shake as if they were ready to collapse underneath her any second. The heat from the fire behind them made her sweat in his blue jean jacket. "How long do you think it'll be before the fire trucks get here?" she asked, handing him the cell phone.

As soon as she spoke, sirens sounded in the distance. Jonas wrapped his arm around her shoulders and pulled her close while his gaze zeroed in on the burning building. "In about a minute."

CR

A sense of relief washed over Deidre when she walked out the screen door with a tray of plastic cups and a pitcher of water for the firefighters. The yard reeked of smoke and wet, charred wood, but at least no more flames flickered in the burned-out barn. Three-fourths of the old building had burned to the ground. The men had spent an hour putting out the flames. The firefighters were currently walking around the debris, lifting pieces of blackened wood with their axes to make sure no more hot spots remained. Jonas and the fire inspector met halfway through the yard and approached the porch together.

Emergency vehicles littered the property, their lights highlighting Jonas' soot-marked face in a red, white and blue kaleidoscope. His gaze locked with her questioning one. "It was deliberately set."

Deidre quickly glanced at the charred stairs, guilt tightening her gut. "I should've been more careful with the fertilizer bag I used this morning. It was heavy so I dragged it out of the barn all the way to the front of the house. I didn't know it had a hole in the bottom until I'd reached the flower bed. The fire must have caught on the fertilizer trail and made its way over to the stairs."

"Don't blame yourself, Miss Nelson. As the sheriff stated, the fire was deliberately set." The fire inspector reached out his leathery hand and shook hers. "Edward Ross, ma'am." He released her hand and pushed his fireman's hat back from his sweaty, black brow. "The arsonist must've used a Molotov cocktail type igniter. We found some melted plastic among the debris. He'd apparently tried to be careful about what material he used... I'm sure he hoped it'd burn up in the fire. We've got proof, but I doubt we can get prints." He paused and glanced at Jonas with an expectant expression. "I saw your men making an impression on the ground below the window where the flames never reached."

Jonas nodded. "Good thing it rained hard last night. The imprint has distinctive markings on the shoe's sole. We're hoping the evidence might make it easier to find the person who did this."

Anger whirled inside Deidre at the near miss with her parents' home. "Who would do such a thing? I know it's the end of the summer and antsy kids get into all kinds of mischief..." She trailed off while she poured a cup of water for Edward then handed the tumbler to him. "Anyway, thank you for your help. I hope you catch the person responsible. My parents will be so relieved, and me for them, that they can put all these pranks behind them."

"We don't know for sure this is connected to the pranks yet." Jonas directed his gaze her way. "This went beyond petty vandalism. Fortunately no animals were in that barn, but what if you'd been asleep when this happened? The fire could've continued to spread to the B&B and you could've been killed."

Her chest tightened at Jonas' scary scenario, but Deidre's mind refused to focus and worry about what could've happened. Instead, as she poured him some water, her heart skipped several beats at the intensity in his tone. She knew his job was to protect, but he almost sounded as if he cared what happened to her, not like the man who'd said he wouldn't get emotionally attached.

She handed him the cup and gave him a half smile. "I'm confident you'll catch the person responsible."

"Damn straight," he replied in a clipped tone while he took her offering. Downing the water in one swift gulp, he handed her the cup. "Which is why I'm going back with the inspector and we're jumping right on this."

He was leaving her?

,Her gaze must've been a little too expressive, because Jonas jerked his head back toward the police cars in the background, their blue and white lights still flashing. "Don't worry. I'm posting an officer to sit outside until further notice."

But he'd misread her. Despite the destruction she'd witnessed tonight, she wasn't worried the person or persons would come back. They'd done their damage. Or maybe the complete sense of calm that seemed to steal over her was because Jonas was so confident he'd catch the guilty party. All she knew was...damn it...*he* was leaving!

Before she could utter a word, Jonas waved over one of his officers. "Jeff, I want you to stay here and watch the house tonight."

"Will do." The short, stocky deputy touched his hat and acknowledged Deidre with a respectful nod.

Jonas clapped the inspector on the shoulder. "Let's go, Edward. You can give me a ride. We've got some work ahead of us."

"Thanks for the water." Edward handed her the cup then led Jonas over to his truck.

"What about Admiral?" Deidre called after Jonas.

"I've phoned my foreman, Harrison. He'll stop by and pick him up in the next half hour."

While disappointment rushed through her at the realization Jonas wouldn't be returning tonight, she worked hard to keep her expression neutral. Damn it, how had she quickly become so desperate to spend as much time as she could with the man?

Chapter Five

"Hey." Jonas' tired voice spoke next to her ear at the same time he pulled her back against his hard chest.

Deidre awoke with a surprised gasp, her heart pounding. But the sensation of Jonas' hard, naked chest sliding against her back while he climbed into bed with her turned her gasp into a sigh of contentment. She gave a sleepy smile and snuggled closer to his warm frame.

After staying outside until the last fireman and police officer left, she cleaned the entire house, took a shower and crawled into bed. She'd lain there for a few hours before sheer exhaustion had finally caused her eyes to close. Glancing at the clock, she blinked at the time—three a.m.—and murmured, "I was so wired I finally fell asleep thirty minutes ago."

When Jonas let out a heavy sigh, she glanced at him over her shoulder. "Hey, what's wrong?"

He kissed her shoulder, but she could tell he was thinking about something. "My brother informed me tonight he'd made his decision to put our ranch and the property on the market."

"What?" Deidre rolled onto her back. "But that property has been in your family for decades. You told me your parents worked so hard to leave a legacy for you and your brother."

Jonas shrugged. "Noah's getting married. He wants to build a house in town."

The frustration in Jonas' eyes, pushed a heavy weight against her chest. This had to be part of the underlying tension she'd noticed in him the past couple of days. "Then buy your brother out."

He ran a finger down the side of her face and gave a half smile. "I offered, but Noah wants top dollar and I can't afford that."

The idea that everything Jonas' parents and Jonas had worked for would be all for nothing made her stomach knot. It wasn't right. And their idyllic spot in the woods, the place they'd connected, would belong to someone else. It felt so very wrong. She placed her hand on his cheek as tears filled her eyes. "I'm so sorry."

He smiled and brushed away a tear that rolled down her temple. "No worries. Life happens."

She noticed his smile didn't quite reach his eyes, but Jonas quickly kissed her palm and changed the subject. "I do have some good news."

"Do you have a lead about tonight's fire?"

"Some. We should know more in the morning when the stores open." Regret laced his voice as his hand moved to her belly and he rolled her back to her side, pulling her body flush with his from shoulder to hip. "I know I promised to keep you up all night long, but this wasn't how I envisioned it."

She laughed softly, enjoying the low register of his voice vibrating against her back. He smelled like oatmeal chocolate chip cookies and fresh soap. Man, she could get used to this. *Better nip this wishful thinking in the bud, woman*, she berated herself.

"Mmmm, I see Jeff isn't really doing his job if you can sneak into my house and climb into bed with me undetected."

"Good thing he's on my payroll." He chuckled as he placed

a tender kiss against her neck. "I sent him home once I got back. Truth is, darlin', I didn't want you staying by yourself, even if Jeff was sitting outside all night."

The man just made her want to crawl all over him. Was it his sexy Texan accent or his protective nature that grabbed her deep in the gut? Both, *and* the man underneath, she admitted to herself.

"Is that the only reason?" she said in a sultry tone. She distinctly remembered brushing against a very impressive erection a second ago. Deidre pushed closer and smiled when he growled in her ear, rubbing his cock against her buttocks.

"Don't tempt me," he warned.

"But that's exactly what I'm doing." She pressed harder, arching her body against him.

His warm hands gripped her hips and held her still. "Baby, God knows, I want your ever-lovin' sweet body, but I purposely didn't bring condoms so I wouldn't be tempted to follow my baser instincts. After a night like tonight, you need your sleep."

Both frustrated and appreciative of his thoughtfulness, Deidre gave a half laugh. "But what did you think I'd want once I got this sexy cowboy lawman in my bed?"

Before she could utter another word, he flipped her over on her back and caged her in with his hands on either side of her head. Leaning on one elbow, he let a seductive laugh escape his lips as he slid his hand down her thin T-shirt and back up the outside of her thigh. "I just said for you not to tempt me. I didn't say I wasn't going to pleasure you. I've thought of little else ever since I had that cock-tease of a brief taste of you in the kitchen."

Deidre's heart beat at a rabbit's pace. In his new position, Jonas' shoulders blocked the hall light, leaving his face in shadows. She wished she could see his expression. Her sex began to pulse and her breasts swelled at the thought of him finally tasting her, teasing her, sucking on her clit. "Well then, cowboy, I would never think to stop a man from his deepest desire." Her hand covered his and she directed his fingers to the bottom of her T-shirt.

Her heart thumped harder as he slowly pulled off her T-shirt then tossed the cotton material on the floor, his gaze never leaving hers.

When Jonas began to massage her calves, she shook her head at the devilish look on his face.

"What's wrong?"

The rasp of desire in his voice made goose bumps form on her skin. She glanced down at his briefs, turned on even more by the sight of his erection jutting against the fitted cotton fabric. "As sexy as I find you in your underwear, I don't want you wearing anything at all."

Tension filled his expression and his nostrils flared. "I'm a man with base impulses. If my cock comes anywhere near your sweet, warm body, I'm going to fill it with mine. It's as primal and fundamental as that."

Jonas' frank comment made her breath catch in her throat. She *wanted* him that out-of-control.

"Take them off." She gave him a siren's smile as she lay back and bent her knees. Putting her feet flat on the bed, she spread her thighs wide. "I think you can hold back."

His gaze locked on her sex as he slipped out of his underwear and tossed them on the floor. When his eyes met hers, his gaze darkened and his expression took on a provocative look. "Are you challenging me?"

The sight of his cock, long and thick, surrounded by dark hair, made her walls clench in excitement. She arched her back so her breasts rose toward him. "You bet your sexy ass I'm challenging you."

Before the words had died from her lips, Jonas' heavy body fell on hers, pressing her to the bed. His hands fisted in her hair and his lips hovered over hers as he laid his erection along her sex. Rubbing the outside ridge of his cock against her wet labia, he said in a husky voice, "It feels like you're on fire, you're so damned hot and slick."

Deidre's pulse thrummed in her ears. She desperately wanted him inside her. Closing the small distance between their mouths, she grabbed his lower lip between her teeth and then applied suction with her lips before allowing gravity to pull her back down to the bed. "That's exactly what I am...on fire. I know your nature. You're always prepared. It's what makes you a good sheriff. Tell me you left your condoms in the car."

He gave her a sheepish grin. "Well, a man can be hopeful."

She raised her eyebrow. "Only if they're within reaching distance, cowboy. Just how fast can you mov—"

Jonas was gone, grabbing up his jeans before she could finish.

Deidre chuckled, her body tingling with anticipation.

She was glad she rolled over to her side to wait for him, because doing so allowed her the sexiest view she'd ever witnessed when he returned—Jonas standing in her doorway, slowly unbuttoning his jeans, an intense look on his face.

She held out her hand and gave him a knowing smile. "Want me to put it on?"

Her question made his cock throb. Jonas quickly stepped out of his jeans and handed her the condom.

She opened the package and sat up on her knees. Her gaze locked with his as her fingers touched the tip of his cock.

As pleasurable sensations slammed through him with each downward brush of her fingers, Jonas had to touch her. He slid his fingers through her hair, enjoying the soft silk. "So beautiful," he murmured.

She finished and wrapped her hand around his erection, pulling him onto the bed.

The tugging sensation and her sultry look made his hips move of their own accord. Their skin touched and he felt like a bull ready to break out of a rodeo chute. Jonas bit back the need to ram his cock deep into her wet heat. God knew, he wanted to with a vengeance. He closed his eyes tight for a second, holding himself over her, trying to regain control. But when Deidre lifted her legs and wrapped them around his hips, bringing her entrance even closer to the tip of his cock, he let loose a growl of sexual frustration.

Capturing her mouth in a hard, demanding kiss, he thrust his tongue deep, intending for his kiss to be aggressive and dominant. Instead of kissing him back, Deidre began to suck on his tongue in seductive, dragging pulls, turning the tables on his dominance. He was the one caught. His sexual urges immediately focused on the sensation in his mouth and the fact there seemed to be a direct tie straight to his cock.

His balls tightened with each tug and pull, and he found himself thinking how good it would feel to have her lips around his erection...just like this...aggressive, never-ending suction. When she ran her tongue around his in one long sweeping lick, a jolt of heated lust swept to his groin like a wildfire spreading in his veins.

Having his cock against her skin but not sliding inside her became a painful, ball-busting, agonizing experience.

Gritting his teeth in order to hold back, Jonas moved his kiss down her jaw and then nibbled at her collarbone before sliding his lips to her breast.

As he circled his tongue around her taut, pink nipple, her moans of approval encouraged him more. Instead of taking the bud into his mouth, he moved to the other breast and treated it to the same attention.

"Jonas, suck them," she begged. She arched her back and her fingernails scraped his shoulders. He fucking loved it...loved being the man to bring out this raw, uninhibited honesty. He wanted to be the man to fulfill her every sexual fantasy...and to delve into new ones together.

He captured her nipple and nipped hard at the bud before sucking the tip deep inside his mouth. Deidre's hips rocked underneath him, a pleased moan rushing past her lips. Jonas flexed his stomach muscles and pressed the hard surface against her slick heat, giving her the friction she sought while relishing each new sound she made. Her hips undulated under him, and the faster pace told him exactly what she wanted.

He slid farther down her body, his hands worshiping her curves and soft skin.

When he placed a gentle kiss on the tuft of blonde hair on her mound, her body stopped moving even though her breathing still continued in soft, sexy gusts.

Jonas glanced up and saw she'd elevated onto her elbows. Her blonde hair was a tangled mess framing her rosy cheeks and swollen lips. Her green-eyed gaze, full of desire, collided with his as he lowered his mouth to her mound and kissed the bit of blonde hair once more.

"How can such a tender kiss make me want to scream?" she said.

The awe in her voice made him kiss her again, but this time slightly lower. The rich, sweet smell of her sex was driving him fucking nuts. "Because you know how very close I am," he replied as he slid his thumbs up her sex and pressed on the outside of her pink skin. His gaze stayed locked with hers while he ran his tongue along her folds.

When her head fell back onto the bed and her legs dropped to the bed, her body's full surrender told him she wanted more. Loving every second of her pleasure, he plunged his tongue inside her core, laving at her enticing flavor. She was a seductive combination of musky sweetness he couldn't describe if he had to. All he knew was her taste made him hard as granite and ache like a virgin teenager.

Sliding his tongue up her entrance, Jonas flicked her clit in teasing circles. "Jonas," she panted as she rocked her hips and ground her sex against his mouth. He mouthed the bit of firm flesh, pressing his lips against it before biting at it gently with his teeth.

Deidre's body jerked and her breathing changed to frantic gasps. "God, Jonas. I can't," she said sitting up slightly to tug on his head and then his shoulders.

"What's wrong? Did I hurt you?"

She continued to pull at him. "I want you inside me. Now!"

He moved to his elbows above her, setting his cock against her entrance. "Are you sure?" he teased, thrusting his hips slightly.

Pulling him down on top of her, she spoke next to his ear, "I was sure the moment you said, 'In another life'."

Jonas froze at her statement. After all these years, she remembered his last words to her. What did that say about her? *It says she's one helluva woman, you jackass, and if you keep her waiting any longer she may just tell you she'd rather wait for you* in another life.

He lifted himself slightly and captured her gaze as he pressed the head of his cock against her entrance. He didn't say a word while he slowly slid inside her, just held her beautiful green gaze. As he seated his erection fully inside her slick, wet, he'd-died-and-gone-to-heaven folds, a sighing whimper crossed her parted lips.

Jonas couldn't resist as he withdrew and sank his cock deep inside her. He nipped at her lower lip then bit it again in a teasing kiss.

Deidre was surprised by this sexy, playful side she didn't expect to see from Jonas. Her easy-going cowboy with the teasing smile had returned. Her heart soaring, she wrapped her arms tight around his shoulders and kissed him hard as she began to rock her hips in a slow, tantalizing rhythm, a sexy counter to his thrusts that sank deep every time he penetrated her.

Jonas' tongue parried with hers in a dominant thrust and pull, moving to the same building momentum of his hips rocking with hers. He was big and heavy, spreading her legs deliciously wide as he moved inside her.

Breathing deep, Deidre started to push him over on his side, but she apparently pushed too far. She let out a yelp of surprise when he went flying down to the floor, taking her with him in the process.

After the initial shock wore off, Jonas' brow furrowed in concern. "You okay, sweetheart?"

Glancing at the tangle of covers beneath them, she grinned. "Good thing you and the covers broke my fall."

Jonas' warm hands clasped her bare buttocks and a sinful smile canted his lips. "Nah, I meant to do this, darlin'." His work-roughened hands grabbed her rear tighter, and he used his hold to press her mound hard against his cock. "I've been dying to see how well you've learned to ride."

"Hmmm, that sounds like a challenge." Deidre kicked the covers off her legs and slid her hands up his chest, enjoying the flex and play of his thick pectorals and the light sprinkle of dark hair under her fingers as she straddled his hips.

Jonas captured her hands and planted a kiss on the beating pulse at each wrist. His gaze heavy with desire, he placed her hands on his shoulders. Running his hands down her sides, he palmed her thighs. "When you ride me, I want to feel every single muscle from here," he squeezed her thigh muscles then ran his hands up her thighs until his thumbs touched her sex, "to here, gripping the hell out of me."

Jonas left her completely speechless. Deidre had never felt sexier and more cherished than she did by the man lying underneath her. Lifting herself up on her knees, she slowly lowered her body down over his shaft until his cock filled her completely.

The full, stretching sensation felt so damn good, she just sat there for several seconds and closed her eyes, savoring the numerous emotions and physical responses running through her. Past yearnings, dream-filled nights, jerking awake sweating and throbbing. Lust, elation, building passion and mutual body heat merged, creating a sense of rightness and completion she couldn't put to words.

She opened her eyes when she felt Jonas' chest rising and falling at a faster pace underneath her hands.

"I'm sure I'm going to like how you ride, but damn, you're beautiful just sitting astride."

She heard the tension in his tone, felt the tightness of his skin under her palms. Jonas was holding back for her. She flexed her inner muscles and grasped his cock in a tight pelvic squeeze. "But then it wouldn't be called riding, would it?" She began to rock her hips in a steadily increasing motion. Every movement jammed him deeper inside her, sending jolts of exquisite pleasure shooting to her sex.

"No, I guess it wouldn't." His voice sounded a bit strained as his fingers dug into her buttocks.

Deidre shivered at the sexy picture he made with his wavy black hair all askew and the muscles in his tan neck flexing in and out. His eyes were half closed, watching her, and his nostrils flared as he took deeper and deeper breaths. Her gaze slid lower to his abs, flexing with each counter thrust of his hips. She decided she liked this position, if nothing else for the great view it gave her of his well-cut, hardworking body.

When he reached up and rubbed her nipples with his thumbs, then tweaked the sensitive pink tips between his fingers, he said, "I'm not planning on coming alone."

"You...you don't have to worry," she stammered as splinters of desire shot down her belly and straight to her sex with each bit of pressure he applied. She dug her fingernails into his shoulders and leaned closer as her climax approached in tighter and tighter spirals of erotic flexes.

Jonas pinched her nipples hard and said in a husky voice, "Nothing compares to the feel of your warm body clasping me tight."

She was so close. The pleasure-pain he applied to her nipples sent tiny shockwaves rippling down her spine, but when he grabbed her hips and thrust upward at the same time he pulled her closer, his body hit just the right spot on her clit. She almost missed his roar of pleasure as he came because her own scream of ecstasy lasted throughout her orgasm.

Thunderous, unrelenting vibrations contracted her walls around him again and again. She rocked against his thick erection, riding her climax until her arms and legs shook so hard she collapsed on his chest.

As her body rose and fell with his heavy breathing, Deidre reveled in the sheen of sweat that coated both their bodies. Jonas ran his fingers across her hair, pushing the damp strands away from her face. She smiled at the tingle of excitement his slight touch evoked within her, knowing she'd never get enough of him. From his strong sense of right and wrong, to the way he made her knees threaten to give way whenever he stepped into the room, the man more than fulfilled every fantasy she'd ever had...and then some.

While his heart rate slowed to its normal pace, Jonas inhaled Deidre's alluring pear-blossom scent. He relished the feel of her weight blanketing him and the sensation of being deep inside her. He could see himself with this woman forever. The thought made his stomach knot and deep-seated mistrust rush to the forefront of his mind. Not to mention fear. He didn't want to be hurt again. He felt so strongly about Deidre, she had the power to destroy him.

He knew Deidre had done nothing to deserve his judgment, but some wounds never healed. She deserved a man who could completely give her his trust and his heart. His body tensed and his grip around her waist tightened at the thought of Deidre kissing, let alone having sex with another man.

She lifted her head, concern etching her brow. "What's wrong?"

His gaze searched hers. "Nothing. I just wish I'd met you eleven years ago."

Her fingers brushed his jaw as a half smile tilted her lips. "Our pasts are just that. Never regret it. Instead, be proud of the decisions you've made. They are the building blocks of who you are."

He gave a self-deprecating laugh. "Yeah, mistrustful, hard,

unyielding."

Surprise lit her gaze. "Is that truly how you see yourself?" Shaking her head, she slid to his side and leaned on her elbow to stare at him. "I see a one-in-a-million man, a man who walked away from a magnetic attraction due to his own moral standards. I see a man whose calculated thinking landed him the well-respected role as the town sheriff."

"A man who will never trust another woman," he interrupted in a cold tone. She didn't need to know fear was the driving factor.

She raised her eyebrow at his narrowed, suspicious gaze. "Really? You wouldn't trust a woman who ached to touch you, who felt your desire, knew you wanted her, a woman who had no personal relationship or binding commitment holding *her* back?"

She rolled away, stood and stared down at him. "Men aren't the only ones who own the right to start a relationship, Jonas." Pointing to her chest, she continued. "This woman walked away because of *her* moral standards."

Before he could respond, she grabbed the shirt he'd tossed onto the chair beside the bed and walked out of the room.

Jonas sat up and rested his elbow on the bed, staring at the open doorway...speechless. Leave it to Deidre to put it all in perspective. He knew he'd fallen in love with her spunky, tell-it-like-it-is self for a reason. He no longer had to deny his attraction to her. She was right. She had walked away and never pursued their mutual attraction. Like him, she'd never forgotten. She had always cared...all these years.

Once he'd pulled on his jeans, he found her in the living room. She stood wearing his shirt, her back to him as she stared out the window. His cock hardened instantly when he mentally acknowledged she was naked beneath his shirt.

His woman.

He approached her and wrapped his arms around her waist. Gathering her close, he nuzzled her neck. "Would an apology for being a complete ass earn your forgiveness?"

She folded her arms over his and sighed. "I can't change the past."

He turned her in his arms and planted a kiss on her forehead, his heart thumping hard. A lump formed in his throat, but he had to ask. "Are you offering me a future?"

She grinned and snaked her arms around his neck. Standing on her tiptoes, she spoke next to his ear in a husky voice, "I know you said you'd never ask a woman to marry you again. If you plan to stick to your vow, because men do silly things sometimes, I hope that you'd at least consider the alternative of accepting a woman's marriage proposal."

Jonas' heart jerked and he set her away so he could meet her gaze. He couldn't dare hope. "Are you asking me to marry you?"

Deidre laughed and shook her head. "No. I'm not. I'm just asking you to consider the possibility that the male isn't the only one who can propose marriage."

Confusion settled within him. As much as her statement made his aversion to commitment and opening himself up to being hurt jump front and center in his mind, his stomach twisted into knots. For a split second he'd experienced joyous acceptance of the idea of having Deidre to himself, 'til death did they part.

A wide grin spread across his face and his spirits lifted as he locked his fingers together at the base of her spine. "If the right woman asked me, I think my answer would be a definite 'yes'."

Grabbing his hand at the small of her back, she laced her

fingers with his, a sexy smile on her face. "I'm glad to hear you're open to the possibility." She tugged him back toward the bedroom. "Now, about that soft bed calling to us..."

Jonas quickly scooped her up in his arms and chuckled at her squeal of surprise. As he carried her into the bedroom, he planted a kiss on her throat. "You really don't think you'll actually sleep in that bed as long as I'm around, do you?"

When she responded with a seductive "I'm counting on it, cowboy", he felt the tension in his chest he'd constantly carried around like a coat of armor start to give way to something akin to relaxation.

Chapter Six

A couple hours later, Jonas awoke to the sound of his cell phone ringing. Dawn's light streaked through the green and white curtains as he quickly got up and pulled his phone from his jeans back pocket.

Flipping open the phone, he glanced at the caller ID and spoke in a low voice. "What do you have, Jeff?"

"Heya, boss. I roused Jamie at Kicks Footwear and got him to check his records. Good thing for us this particular style of shoe was recently released in the market. Because the manufacturer offers a lifetime warranty, the store keeps track of sales. Only three people have bought the boys' tennis shoes that match both the size and the shoe tread we lifted near the barn."

Jonas straightened his spine as he shifted to sheriff mode. "Give them to me."

"Joey Randall, Chaz Blackstone and Aaron Shomar." Jeff paused for a second and continued. "Motive and connection come to mind. Know what I'm thinking, sir?"

Jonas' gaze narrowed. The Blackstones owned the Blackstone B&B that had opened in town a little over a year ago. He knew the Blackstones friendly with Deidre's parents, but their son Chaz was a bit of a hothead. There was only one way to find out if he was responsible for the vandalism and destruction on the Flying Wind property. "I think we're both on the same page. I'll stop by and pick you up on the way to the Blackstone B&B."

"Think Chaz'll be up that early?"

Anger festered within him at the thought Deidre could've been hurt because of a teenager's stunt. "I don't give a rat's ass if he's up that early or not," he shot back before he closed the cell phone with a determined snap.

"You have to go."

Deidre's sleepy voice drew his attention. She looked so sexy sitting up on her elbow, her tangled, wavy blonde hair framing her face. Understanding reflected in her green gaze as she held the sheet around her breasts and stared at him intently.

Jonas nodded while pulling on his underwear. "We're chasing down a lead in yesterday's fire."

Deidre sat up, her expression alert. "I hope you find who did this. I really don't want to leave my parents behind with someone still lurking out there who's elevated his pranks to deadly activities."

Jonas' heart constricted at her casual mention of leaving. "Your parents will be back today?" Damn, he'd been so caught up in Deidre, he'd lost track of time.

She nodded.

Mixed emotions shifted within him like a sandcastle being eaten by the ebb and flow of an inevitable incoming tide. While he shrugged into his jeans and shirt, his gut told him to ask her to stay, but old wounds kept the words locked deep inside.

Setting his jaw, he gave her a curt nod. "I'll have a report to them by the end of the day."

A half smile curved her lips. Sexual tension and unspoken words flowed between them while they stared at each other for several seconds.

She tilted her head as if she sensed the internal battle going on in his head. "You'd better get going."

Snapping to attention, Jonas squared his shoulders and pulled on his socks before stepping into his boots. He turned to go, but cast his gaze back her way. Before he could speak, she made a shooing motion with her hand. "Go."

Jonas grabbed his Stetson from the dresser and set it firmly on his head. As he walked out of the room, she called after him, "The sheriff always gets his man."

And his woman, he finished mentally. As he made his way out of the house, a broad smile spread across his face. And it felt damn good.

CR

"Can you believe he's up at this hour?" Jeff sounded surprised as Jonas drove down the Blackstones' asphalt drive toward the bed and breakfast ranch house.

Chaz Blackstone tugged his baggy jeans shorts back up his lanky form as he stood up from a crouched position at the edge of the drive. He dipped his paintbrush into a can of white paint then applied a new coat to one of the wrought iron spindles on the fence that curved in a semicircle around the entrance to the B&B.

When Jonas turned into the drive, Chaz glanced their way. Adjusting his navy blue baseball hat, he squinted against the bright morning sun.

Once he turned off the car engine, Jonas handed Jeff the folder that was on the seat between them and got out of the car.

"Mornin', Sheriff." Chaz touched his hat's bill and stared at his visitors, paintbrush paused in midair next to the fence. "My parents are inside preparing the morning meal for their guests."

"Being punished?" Jonas asked as he glanced at the gallon can of paint next to Chaz's tennis shoes. While his gaze was averted, he surreptitiously examined the teenager's athletic shoes. Sure enough, they matched the picture of the brand the Kicks Footwear's manager said was in high demand with the lifetime warranty.

"Nah, just making the place look nice." Chaz returned to his work, swiping his brush along the thin wrought-iron post.

Jonas caught Jeff's nod toward Chaz's shoes. He raised his eyebrow to let the deputy know he saw them. Now, to get the kid to willingly show him the bottom of his right shoe. "You been working hard around here this weekend?"

Chaz paused his brush strokes for a second. "Yeah, helping my parents with the upkeep," he commented before he bent and wiped more paint on his brush from the can.

A few drops of white paint landed on the black asphalt as he returned the brush to the fence, giving Jonas an idea.

He stepped right beside Chaz and kicked the nearly full can of paint as he pretended to inspect the boy's handiwork. "Nice job, son." Satisfied that enough of the white paint had sloshed over the side of the can and onto the pavement, he asked in a casual tone, "You didn't go out at all yesterday?"

"Huh?" Chaz stopped painting and glanced at him, wrinkling his freckled nose.

Jonas was determined to draw the kid out. "Did you go anywhere yesterday?"

Chaz shrugged then dipped his paintbrush once more. "I went to the store for my mom to pick up some bacon, milk and eggs." Straightening, he stepped around Jonas and began working on another part of the fence.

Jonas glanced down at the asphalt and a heavy dose of anger washed over him at the sight of Chaz's shoeprint perfectly stamped in white wet paint against the black drive.

"You should really be more careful," Jonas said as he reached over and pulled the manila folder out from under Jeff's arm.

"What are you talking abou—" Chaz cut himself off when his gaze landed on the perfect white shoeprints he'd made on the pavement. Lifting his shoe, he stared at the paint now coating the bottom. "Shit, my parents are going to freak at this mess!"

Jonas pulled out a photo of the impression they'd taken and tossed it on the ground next to the print on the asphalt. A kind of sad satisfaction swept through him that the photo was an exact match, all the way down to the nicked outer edge of the sole. "There's one thing you're definitely right about. Your parents are going to freak."

Pointing to the photo, Jonas continued. "This impression was taken at the scene of a crime last night, next to an old barn on the Flying Wind's property. The barn almost burned to the ground, Chaz. The fire spread to the house, engulfing the stairs. Had we not caught it in time, it probably would've burned the entire B&B, too. Know anything about that?"

"I don't know what you're talking about." Despite his denial, when Chaz's anxious gaze met his, Jonas noted how pale the teenager's skin suddenly looked underneath the heavy sprinkle of freckles across his nose.

Retrieving the photo, Jonas slid it back inside the folder and handed the package to Jeff at the same time he pulled his handcuffs from the leather snap on his gun belt. He took a step forward and gripped Chaz's wrist, slapping the handcuff on him.

"You have the right to remain silent."

The kid's strawberry-blond eyebrows rose and his eyes widened in fear as Jonas took the paintbrush out of his free hand and gave it to his deputy. Locking the second cuff on the boy's other wrist, he said, "Jeff, please go get the Blackstones."

As Jeff walked toward the house, Jonas continued with his Miranda warning. "Anything you say can and will be used against you—"

"Wait!" Chaz jerked around, his expression panicked. "You can't arrest me. I didn't mean to burn the house, just that old ratty barn they planned to tear down anyway." He hung his head and continued in a lower voice, "I thought if the Flying Wind had lots of problems... I just wanted people to come to our B&B."

Disappointment tensed Jonas' shoulders and he shook his head at the kid's illogical thinking. "You could've killed someone, Chaz." Gripping the boy's upper arm in a firm hold, he glanced up to see Roger and Joyce Blackstone running down the porch stairs toward them.

"Why in the world are you arresting our son?" Chaz's father asked while his mother clung to her husband's arm.

Jonas met their concerned gazes. "Let's all head to the office and discuss it there."

❧

Jonas drove up to the Flying Wind B&B as the sun slid lower in the sky. He'd spent the entire day at the office filling out paperwork. Once he talked to the Nelsons, he could wrap up the Blackstone case completely.

Deidre's mother and father came out on their front porch

as he got out of his car.

Jonas walked up to the stairs and brushed the rim of his hat. "Evening, Glen and Dot. How was your trip?"

"Wonderful." Dot's skin was a little darker than when they'd left and there was a definite spark in her deep blue eyes.

Glen stepped down the stairs and shook Jonas' hand. "We just got off the phone with the Blackstones. They were very shocked and apologetic about their son's behavior. I wanted to talk to you about Chaz's punishment, Sheriff."

"I'm not done with my report—" Jonas cut himself off with a sigh, knowing small town ways of ignoring protocol were ingrained and the hardest to get past when it came to his job. Releasing Glen's hand, he put his booted foot up on the burned bottom step and prepared to negotiate with the older couple. "He needs a good lickin', in my opinion."

Glen walked back up to stand beside his wife. Folding his arms, he set his mouth in a determined line. "I seem to remember a certain young cowboy who came to work at this B&B a little over ten years ago. From what I remember, his daddy said he was headstrong and had a wild streak. He hoped that by working for us, we'd straighten his son out."

Jonas mirrored Glen's pose, crossing his arms over his chest as he stared the older man down. Glen had been more than an employer. He'd been a mentor in many ways. "Are you telling me you don't plan to press charges? Deidre could've been killed if the fire had continued to spread."

Regret softened Glen's stern features for a brief second. "No, we're not pressing charges on the condition that Chaz makes up for what he's done. We're thankful you held up to your word and kept watch after the B&B and our daughter."

Jonas could tell Glen wasn't going to back down from his stance on the Chaz issue. Preparing himself to push for the harshest punishment he could get the Nelsons to agree to, he met Glen's steady gaze. "I'm thinking community hours. Lots of community hours." He glanced at the burned-out barn and then shifted his line of sight to the step under his foot. "After he helps clean up this mess."

"Agreed." Glen nodded then added, "And we think he should have to help out at the station as well."

Jonas stiffened. "The station?"

"That way you can keep an eye on him and point him in the right direction. I'm sure you could use an extra worker around the office," Dot added, her short dark hair bobbing as she nodded her agreement.

The Nelsons had effectively backed him into a corner he saw no way around. Jonas rolled his head from shoulder to shoulder in frustration.

"What do you say, Jonas?"

When Glen called him by his first name instead of "sheriff", the older man was definitely playing upon their longstanding friendship. Inclining his head in grudging approval, Jonas lowered his arms and relaxed his shoulders now that they'd come to an agreement.

Glen gave a big smile. "Good, glad we got that out of the way. I wanted to talk to you about purchasing a portion of your property to expand the B&B trails and possibly add a couple guest cabins in the future. My Deidre said there's some fine land back there."

If Glen bought some of his property, he should be able to afford to give Noah the price he wanted. His brother might not want the work of owning a ranch, but he'd want to bring his future children to visit the family ranch later in life. Jonas' spirits soared.

Jonas nodded, but kept his expression neutral. "Let me

talk to Noah and see if he's agreeable."

"Sounds good." The older man crossed his arms, looking very proud of himself.

This was Deidre's doin'. Jonas cast his gaze through the screen door. Why hadn't she come out with her parents? "Can I speak to Deidre for a few minutes?"

"She left a half hour ago," Dot said.

Surprise shot through him. Was helping him her parting gift? "Did she leave a note?"

Dot's eyes lit up. "She did say, 'Tell Jonas I'll see him'."

Dejection hit him hard, making him feel sick to his stomach. Deidre's parents must've noticed his tanking mood because both Glen and Dot stared at him as if waiting for him to say something.

Jonas cleared his throat and touched his hat once more. "I'll be in touch with you once I talk to Noah, and to set up a work schedule for Chaz."

Glen smiled and wrapped his arm around his wife's shoulders. "We're here when you're ready. Have a great evening."

ॐ

Jonas headed up the long drive leading to his ranch, feeling as if a two-hundred-pound weight had fallen on his chest. When his gaze landed on a familiar blue compact rental car sitting in his driveway, his spirits rose. Deidre hadn't left. Enjoying the euphoric feeling, he parked his car and turned off the engine.

Deidre sat on the top step of his porch, one leg crossed over the other as she leaned back on her arms. Her pink tank top pulled tight against her breasts while her sandaled foot swung casually underneath a long prairie skirt. She smiled and stood as he got out of the car and shut the door.

"Evening, Sheriff."

Jonas didn't say a word. Instead, he mounted the stairs two at a time until he stood in front of his woman. She'd tried to help him save his ranch. He could get used to the sight of her sitting on the stairs waiting for him to get home, the last remnants of sun casting a golden glow across her bare shoulders. When he stared down at her upturned face and her smile broadened, he realized just how much she'd come to mean to him, how much she'd always meant to him.

"Your dad offered to buy some of my land," he said.

She tilted her head to the side. "He did, did he?"

Jonas nodded, his heart beating double-time as he waited for her to admit she'd had a part in it.

Instead, she stayed quiet and they just stared at one another for several seconds until she finally stood and brushed off her skirt. "I couldn't leave without saying goodbye."

Jonas' stomach pitched. She was really leaving? Instead of saying what was in his heart, his self-preservation defenses kicked in, lodging the words in his throat. Stepping into her personal space, he rubbed a strand of her hair between his fingers. "I'd say our reunion warranted a personal goodbye." The floral scent that rose from the silky strands made his groin jump to instant attention, rekindling memories of their night together. Jonas swallowed the lump that formed in his throat at the thought of her driving away, the idea he'd never see her, touch her or make love to her again.

Sliding his hand under her hair, he cupped the back of her neck and pulled her toward him until her chest touched his. Her lips drew his like a magnet. "I'm going to miss this sexy mouth."

Deidre's heart pounded against his chest and her smile faltered. When her gaze dropped to his mouth and her tongue darted out to wet her own lips, Jonas couldn't resist her nonverbal invitation. "Dee, I—" His hand tightened around her waist and his mouth covered hers. He kissed her with all the love he felt but couldn't put into words.

The passionate intensity of Jonas' kiss thrilled Deidre. But she knew in her heart he was holding back.

Her heart also ached at the knowledge he couldn't see beyond his past to tell her how he felt. She knew deep inside, hurt drove him. The fact he'd let her go instead of taking a chance on them felt as if someone had just ripped her chest open. Placing her hand on his jaw, she broke their kiss and searched his hooded gaze.

Her stomach flip-flopped at the sensation of his evening whiskers brushing against her fingers. A pleasant burn remained on her lips from the recent contact. She wanted to beg him to ask her to stay, to trust his heart to her. She wanted to tell him she'd been in love with him for ten years, but the words wouldn't come.

As if he knew she wanted more than he could ever give, Jonas' dark, hungry eyes drank in her features. Was he trying to memorize them to keep them with him forever? He didn't say a word, just lowered his head toward hers once more.

Before she blurted her feelings for him in an embarrassing emotional outburst, she stepped out of his embrace. "I'll see you, Jonas."

Deidre started to walk down the first stair, her legs shaking.

A strong hand encircled her upper arm. Jonas turned her

around and hauled her against his chest. "You're just going to walk away?" Anger reflected in his voice while bewilderment filled his deep blue gaze.

Deidre's heart thumped at his adamant question. The man needed to let go of his past if they ever had a chance of a future together. She was willing to gamble. The question was...was he?

"You made it very clear you have little to give." She stood on her toes and kissed him on the cheek then pulled free of his hold. "I'll always remember our time together with a smile on my face."

Jonas' jaw ticced as he grasped her upper arms in a firm hold. "Don't you want to find out where this goes?"

Deidre met his intense gaze, her heart racing in a full gallop. "Don't you know that having a relationship means you take risks? That you open up your heart, fully knowing it could be broken?"

His grip on her arms tightened and an incredulous expression crossed his face as realization dawned. "Are you going to walk away from us?"

She just stared at him, letting him believe what he wanted. It took all her internal willpower not to throw herself into his arms, to make her body do what her mind demanded, while her heart screamed the opposite, but Deidre was fighting for her man...for a strong future together.

Emotions ranging from hurt to anger stormed in his gaze. Jonas shook her gently. "Don't you know that I love you, Dee? I've always loved you. I want to spend more time together and see where this takes us."

Her heart soared with happiness at his words. Tears filled her eyes, spilling down her cheeks. "Are you willing to take the risk and open up your heart again?"

He yanked her to his chest and cupped the back of her

head, pressing her cheek against his neck. "God, yes. I'm asking you to stay. I don't think I'd be a complete man without you, sweetheart."

Deidre wrapped her arms around his waist and hugged him tight as she sobbed with happiness against his neck. "I've always loved you, and I always will."

Stepping back, she wiped her tears and pulled out a piece of paper from a pocket in her skirt. "Here's my schedule. Can you pick me up?"

Jonas took the paper and read over the flight itinerary, then jerked his gaze to hers. "This is a round trip ticket."

She nodded. "It is. I'm going home to close up my apartment through the winter. My parents have decided they want to do a lot more traveling, and they want to spend their Christmas in Texas." She smiled. "They can't do this without me, so I told them I'd help out and even spruce up their menu during my stay."

His gaze narrowed. "You weren't really leaving?"

"My return to Ventura will only be temporary."

Jonas' dark eyebrows drew down in a stern look. "Unless someone convinces you to stay, right?"

Deidre shook her head slowly. "No, unless someone gives me a *reason* to stay."

Jonas stepped close. Unrestrained love welled in his chest. "I'll spend the rest of our lives together making up for all the lost years."

She laughed and brushed her lips softly against his. "Don't make promises unless you plan to keep them, cowboy. Then again," she unsnapped his handcuffs from his belt, and stepped away, continuing in a light tone. "There's something to be said for anticipation."

Jonas watched in surprise as she pulled a baggie of cookie dough out of her pocket and waved the handcuffs and the sweet treat suggestively in front of him.

He reached for her, but she evaded his grasp and took off down the stairs, casting a flirty, come-hither look over her shoulder. In a swirl of a chambray prairie skirt, she disappeared around the corner of his home.

He glanced at the flight itinerary in his hand. Deidre had a couple hours before she had to be at the airport.

"And when I convince you to say 'I do', I'm going to enjoy chasing and catching you for the rest of my days," he said with a wicked grin as he took off after his woman.

Anticipation... Hell yeah!

Susanna's Seduction

Dedication

Thank you to my Patrice Michelle Yahoo group readers for walking through this book a chapter at a time with me. Thanks for all your wonderful support!

To my family for supporting my crazy writing hours. I love you!

Acknowledgements

To my critique partners Cheyenne McCray and Rhyannon Byrd and my editor Linda Ingmanson...thank you for helping make Susanna's Seduction an even better story.

Chapter One

Always the bridesmaid, Susan thought as a wry smile formed on her lips. Crisp fall wind ruffled her hair, blowing the long, blonde strands around her shoulders. She stood staring at the black granite sign outside an upscale Italian restaurant in East Hampton. *Piccoli's,* the fancy, gold letters read.

Why in the world have I let Jason talk me into being "the heavy"?

She knew why. He was her baby brother and she felt responsible for Jason, even if he was now twenty-seven and about to get married.

A few weeks ago, during a luncheon with Jason and Melanie, his bride-to-be asked Susan to be her maid of honor in her "Melanie-ish" sort of way.

"Oh, Susan, could you please be my maid of honor? I would ask one of my friends to do it, but they're all so flighty. You've been a bridesmaid in so many weddings; you're a real pro at this. You're so sensible, Susan. I know you'd do an awesome job."

Susan didn't care for the indirect implication Melanie made—that she was "always the bridesmaid, but never the bride". She was about to decline when Jason piped in, "Come on, Susan. Do it for me?" He gave her those puppy dog eyes, stopping the "no thanks" on her lips.

When she'd first met Melanie, Susan wondered how the socialite and Jason had ended up together. Jason didn't run in the same social circles as Melanie. Melanie was a debutante through and through. Susan could only surmise it must be "true love" for Melanie. By the look in Jason's eyes when he shifted his gaze back to his fiancée, she knew it was for her brother. Against her better judgment, she heard herself saying, "Okay."

She should've listened to her reservations about accepting the task of maid of honor. This morning, Jason called her at work.

"Susan, I need your help. Melanie just received a fax from Piccoli's. The rehearsal dinner is in two days and she's in a panic because the menu isn't correct. She asked if you could handle talking to the restaurant manager and get this straightened out."

Susan sighed. "Why can't she call them herself?"

Jason laughed and whispered into the phone, "To be honest, I think she's a little intimidated. According to her, Piccoli's is the place to be seen in East Hampton and I think she wants to make sure she doesn't step on any toes."

"Oh, great, but it's okay for me to go in raging?" She snorted into the phone. Granted, she didn't personally frequent the restaurants in East Hampton, so she had nothing to lose, but it was the sheer principle that raised her ire.

"Come on, Sensible Susan," Jason cajoled.

She set her teeth. He'd taken to calling her that ever since their luncheon. "Jason, I don't appreciate the nickname—"

"I know, I know," he interrupted, snickering at her irritation as only a younger brother could. "But you're very good with people. After all, you didn't get to be the top public relations person in your firm by accident. This is the last request. I promise."

And here I stand. Susan shook her head and glanced at the faxed copy of the rehearsal dinner's menu in her hand. Opening the door to Piccoli's, she muttered, "Here goes nothing."

After she spoke to the waiter, she pulled out a chair at a nearby table and sat down to wait for him to get the manager. She was glad she'd picked early morning to accomplish her task, for the restaurant was currently empty. It would make for an easier discussion if she didn't have to worry about the patrons overhearing their conversation.

"How can I help you, Miss?"

Susan turned at the deep, masculine voice. She stood and extended her hand. "Susan Brennon."

Her heart thumped as the handsome man grasped her hand in his warm one. His chocolate brown eyes surveyed her face while his sensual mouth curved into a smile. The faint, arousing smell of aftershave tickled her nose, making her want to pull closer and take a stronger whiff. He didn't release her hand right away and tiny bolts of electricity shot up her arm. Her pulse thrummed at the sensation.

She let go of his hand then ran her fingers through her wind-blown hair, trying to smooth it. Handing him the corrected menu, she launched into her purpose for being there. "My future sister-in-law asked me to talk to you about the errors in the menu for her rehearsal dinner."

He raised a dark eyebrow, amusement reflected in his gaze. "Sent you to the wolves, did she?"

Susan laughed. "I hope not." More like the lion's den, she thought as she watched his dark head bend over the menu. He was tall and had the sexiest hands she'd ever seen. Neatly trimmed nails topped squared fingers and broad palms. She hadn't detected much of an accent when he'd spoken, but his pitch-black hair and olive skin tone made her wonder if he was Italian. Charcoal gray dress slacks and a black, fine-gauge sweater hugged his physically fit physique well.

He looked up, his expression apologetic. "Please forgive the error, Miss Brennon. I'm sure this can be corrected."

Susan smiled. "Thank you for your help...I'm sorry, I didn't get your name."

He extended his hand again and took her hand in his. "Michael." The electricity was back and her heart tripped several beats when his dark eyes fixed on hers. "You know, I'll bet I can even get a few bottles of wine thrown in."

"Really?" she asked, surprised.

"If you'll have dinner with me on Friday night."

Her stomach tumbled and her cheeks heated at his close scrutiny. "Is that a bribe?" She gave him a half smile while trying to regain her composure.

"Absolutely."

The sensation of his lips brushing against her knuckles made her body hum all over. After a few seconds, her brain reengaged, and the day he'd suggested for their date finally sank in. Disappointment made her growing anticipation plummet. "Wait...Friday night? That's the night of the rehearsal dinner."

His eyebrows drew together. "Do you have a date?"

"No, I—"

"Well then, it's settled. I'll be your date," he finished with a pleased smile.

"You don't have to work?" This was moving faster than she expected.

"No, I have that night off." His eyes twinkled and his grin broadened.

Susan thought about Jason's latest nickname for her. She *had* been sensible all her life, at least when it came to dating men. She'd always dated guys she could read—the most sensible kind—and as a result had had the most sensible relationships...which led to boredom.

Michael was a total stranger, but beyond the attraction *he* was a mystery. She could meet him here at the restaurant, along with the rest of the wedding party. No harm in that. She smiled up at him.

"Sure, why not."

ᘓ

Susan stood outside Piccoli's trying not to look like she was expecting anyone. After all, what if Michael didn't show? She was soaking in the last warm rays of the setting sun when a sudden cold wind sailed through the parking lot. Her black silk knee-length dress did little to keep her warm, so she tugged her overcoat tight around her body and absorbed the wool's thick warmth. Jason passed her on the way back from his car, carrying Melanie's camera. He held the door open for her. "Coming, sis?"

She quickly glanced up one side of the parking lot then down the other. Nothing. Turning toward the open door, she shook off her sinking spirits. "Yeah, just getting some fresh air."

She followed her brother through the dimly lit, cozy restaurant. Smells of rich marinara sauce, garlic and steaming bread met her senses. Her heels made no sound on the deep red carpet as they walked past several tables with starched white tablecloths until they reached the large private room reserved for the rehearsal dinner guests. A long table housed the entire entourage of bridesmaids and groomsmen as well as

Melanie's parents. Susan wished her parents were still alive so they could experience this evening with them.

After she handed her coat to the waiter, she settled into the plush leather seat next to Jason and smiled so no one would notice her melancholy mood.

"Oh, my gosh!" Melanie gushed, awe in her voice. She grabbed Jason's arm and peered out into the restaurant. "Mr. Piccoli is coming over to speak to us. I can't believe it. Maybe he's going to apologize for the menu mix up."

Susan forgot all about Mr. Piccoli when she saw Michael approaching the open door. He smiled as he entered the room, walked to her side of the table and put his hands on the chair next to her.

"I'm sorry I'm late, Susan."

Smiling up at him, Susan turned to introduce him to Jason when she realized she didn't know his last name. Embarrassed heat stained her cheeks. She locked gazes with her brother, hoping a great excuse would come to mind.

Michael took care of her dilemma when he offered his hand to Jason. "Michael Piccoli. Nice to meet you."

At the look of surprise on Melanie's face, Susan had to laugh, even though she was just as shocked to discover her date was none other than the famous restaurant's owner.

"How did you two meet?" Melanie's curious gaze darted between Susan and Michael.

Michael turned his warm brown eyes to Susan's upturned face. "I guess you could say we met over a meal, and I've been head over heels ever since."

While Michael pulled out his chair, Jason leaned over and whispered into his sister's ear, "Not so sensible now, huh, sis?"

Jason knew that East Hampton restaurants weren't places

she normally frequented. He had to have guessed she'd just met Michael. Butterflies fluttered in her stomach as she muttered, "Not a word."

Once Michael settled into his seat, Susan shifted her gaze back to her date. His eyes shining with amusement, he leaned close to her ear and said in a low voice, "I hope to go on a 'real' date sometime soon, Susanna."

Susan couldn't help the smile that tilted her lips at the nickname he'd given her. Susanna sounded beautiful coming from him and nowhere near as "sensible" as Susan.

When Michael lifted her hand and planted a tender kiss on her open palm, his penetrating gaze full of seductive promises, her breath caught in her throat. For once in her life, she was happy to just be the bridesmaid.

Dinner flew by much too quickly for Susan. Near the end of the meal, Melanie insisted Michael tell how Piccoli's got started.

He graciously told his story.

"I started with very modest means and nothing but my ambition and a dream. For years I worked in the kitchens of several local restaurants, learning everything I could from the chefs. Eventually, I worked my way up to head chef at an exclusive restaurant, but I craved more. I wanted total control. Basically," he said with a smile, "I wanted to run my own restaurant. Then, one day, as I was doing my rounds in the restaurant, making sure customers were happy with their meals, a customer stopped me and told me how impressed he was with my customer-centered attitude. He offered to back me financially if I wanted to start my own restaurant." Michael grinned, glancing Susan's way before continuing. "I was floored by the man's generous offer. I agreed, and that's how Piccoli's came into existence."

"I guess you bought out the original investor a long time

ago," Melanie added with a laugh as she picked up her glass of wine.

Michael turned her way. "Actually, no."

Her blonde eyebrows rose in surprise. "Surely with the tremendous success of your restaurant, you could've bought him out several times over."

He gave her a half smile. "Yes, but that wasn't the point. This man believed in me. I owed him a great deal. He allowed me to achieve my dream. To this day, he still remains a silent partner of Piccoli's."

Susan's respect for Michael jumped a hundredfold at his response. This was a man of integrity, a man who not only ran his business with his head, but he didn't leave the heart part behind.

She'd seen it happen often. In the cutthroat world of advertising, she'd definitely been on the receiving end of ladder-climbing, back-stabbing co-workers out for "number one" no matter who they had to step on to get there. Crossing over into public relations was the best thing she ever did. She'd found her niche, worked hard to earn her partner status and held her position with an iron fist—all while keeping her integrity intact. At the end of every day, she could still look herself in the mirror and like the person staring back.

Still, there were times when she couldn't help but feel like something was missing in her life. It would be nice to have someone to share her day with.

She came out of her reverie to see Michael looking at her. She smiled, thinking, *I really like this man.*

The wedding party had resumed normal across-the-table chit-chat. She tilted her head as Michael continued to stare.

"What are you thinking?" she asked in a quiet voice.

"That I'm a very lucky man," he replied, his eyes searching her face.

"I think people make their own luck. It sounds like that's exactly what happened when you started and then made a success of Piccoli's."

"I wasn't referring to my restaurant, Susanna. I meant every word of what I said about how we met."

She thought back to his "head of heels" comment and her eyes widened.

"I...uh...thought you were just making a joke."

Michael started to speak when Melanie interrupted them. "Thank you for coming tonight, Susan and Michael. Several of us are going over to Tease for drinks and some dancing, so I guess we'll see you tomo—"

"You'll see us there," Michael finished for her.

A surprised look crossed Melanie's face. "Oh, I didn't think you guys would be interested in coming."

Meaning: I thought you two were too old to hang with us, Susan translated with a mental snort. Though she was surprised Michael wanted to go to Tease.

Susan glanced at him. "You want to go?"

His black eyebrows rose. "We could always go back to my place—"

"We'll see you there," she replied to Melanie, her heart palpitating at the idea of being alone with this seductive man...er, stranger, she reminded herself. She didn't think she was ready to be one-on-one with Michael just yet.

"Then, I guess we'll see you guys there." Melanie rose from her seat and put her purse on her shoulder.

Jason stood, grinning. "See you later, sis."

When they walked away, Michael clasped her hand and

101

kissed the back of it, saying with a chuckle, "You're not afraid to be alone with me, are you?"

"No," she said quickly, glancing up at him.

He gave her a knowing smile then said in a light tone, "Come on. We old people need to keep up with them young whippersnappers."

℃

Michael followed her utility vehicle in his low-slung silver sports car over to the nightclub. Susan shivered when he put his hand on the small of her back to escort her inside. Once they entered the trendy nightclub with its dim ambiance and upbeat music playing in the background, she spied Jason and Melanie sitting among their friends in a circular corner booth.

Jason waved and Michael acknowledged him with a nod. At the same time he clasped her elbow and steered her toward the dance floor, whispering in her ear, "Since you're avoiding being alone with me, I have a confession to make."

Susan started to deny the first part of his comment, but the last half intrigued her. She allowed him to pull her up on the raised, lighted dance floor and deep into the crowd of gyrating dancers before she called out over the music, "What's your confession?"

He gave her a devilish smile then clasped her waist and pulled her fully against his chest. Leaning close, he said in a husky tone, "I see dancing as a form of foreplay...a way to seduce you into wanting to come home with me."

Heat suffused her cheeks and shot straight to her toes as she met his gaze. Raw desire flickered in the murky depths. Swiftly turning in his arms to face away from him, she rocked her hips to the song's fast beat, calling over her shoulder, "I don't go home with strangers."

Michael placed his hand on her waist and pulled her flush against his body. "Then I'll just have to make sure I'm no stranger to you before we leave this dance floor," he murmured against her ear as he spread his fingers wide and lowered his hand. The DJ started up a seductive song at the same time Michael applied pressure against her lower belly. He molded her entire backside to his hard frame, cradling her hips against his.

The crush of the people dancing all around, bumping and jostling them, while Michael held her in such an intimate embrace, literally seducing her in a crowd, turned her breathing shallow and rapid. When his lips grazed her neck, she found herself laying her head against his broad shoulders. *Damn the seductive man.* "I—I barely know you."

Michael's mouth touched the sensitive spot behind her ear. "I'm your knight in shining armor, the man who wants to sweep you off your feet." His erection nudged her buttocks, making her body throb in heated anticipation.

She turned in his arms and put a bit of space between them, giving him a knowing look. "And right into your bed."

Michael gripped her waist and yanked her close, the look on his handsome face intense. "I won't deny my attraction to you."

Her heart skipped a beat at his adamant comment. She looped her arms around his neck as his hands slid to her hips and his rock-hard thigh moved her skirt higher. He fit himself to her like a puzzle piece and tightened his hold, forcing her hips to move with his and the beat of the music.

"But I'm a man who enjoys foreplay just as much as the sexual act. You're beautiful inside and out. I look forward to seducing your mind as well as your body."

His mouth hovered over hers, close enough to kiss her. Susan's pulse thundered in her ears as she glanced at his very kissable mouth. Her instincts told her he had the kind of mouth that could be both hard and hot, depending on his intensity. She liked the idea of the dual scenarios pressing against her, but she wanted him to make the first move.

The alluring music stopped, pulling her out of the seductive moment. She lowered her arms and stepped back, expelling the breath of anticipation she'd been holding.

At the awkward pause between them, her stomach tensed. Things were moving faster with Michael than they ever had with any other man. The pace sent her senses reeling. She turned to walk away. "How about a drink?"

Michael clasped her hand, his expression determined. "Before you walk off this floor, I want to hear you say it, Susanna."

"Say what?" Unable to meet his gaze, she glanced down at his hand holding hers. She noted the difference in his olive complexion next to her fairer skin. Excitement skittered through her at his touch...and the thought of those dark hands skimming up her pale thighs. When he squeezed her fingers slightly, her gaze traveled up his expensive charcoal gray suit until she met his steady gaze.

His thumb rubbed back and forth along the top of her hand while his piercing eyes, unwavering and confident, locked with hers. "That I don't feel like a stranger to you."

Chapter Two

Susan grinned and gave him a neutral answer. "You certainly don't act like a stranger."

A challenging gleam flickered in his eyes. "That's not the answer I was looking for."

"Don't expect me to ever be predictable." She pulled her hand from his and turned to walk off the dance floor. Wow, she enjoyed the back and forth verbal foreplay between them, soaked it up. She did speak the truth. Nothing she'd done so far with Michael was anything her "old" self would've done.

He came up beside her and wrapped his arm around her waist, a sexy smile canting his lips. "I'm counting on that unpredictability, but there is one thing I can predict."

"What's that?" she asked as they walked together between the tables.

"You'll taste as good as a fine merlot."

Heat shot straight to her core at his intimate words. Susan resisted a shiver as he led her over to the bar.

☙

As Michael ordered them a bottle of merlot, Susanna took a few minutes to speak to her brother and his fiancée. Michael's gaze traced the curve of her hips, and he smiled when carnal thoughts quickly followed.

"Your wine, sir?" the bartender asked, drawing his attention as he poured a bit of wine into his glass.

Michael swirled the merlot and inhaled the different scents while his thoughts remained on Susanna. Nodding his approval to the bartender to pour two glasses from the bottle, he set his jaw and forced himself to tamp down his intense desire for this woman.

His relationship with his ex-girlfriend Julie had moved at a velocity even he couldn't have seen with the naked eye. He was a passionate man who approached everything in life with a zealousness and verve others envied. He wanted to follow his lustful instincts with Susanna, but warning bells rang with vivid clarity in his head. He didn't want a repeat of his last relationship and the ones that came before...all fire and no substance.

Susanna was different. When she came to his restaurant to help out Melanie, he figured she'd done it to help her brother. At the dinner tonight, he could tell Jason and Susanna were close, and considering their parents weren't at the rehearsal dinner, he assumed they only had each other. Family came first for him. They always had. He could tell family was very important to her, too.

He watched her talking with Jason and Melanie's friends. She had an infectious smile and exuded quiet confidence, yet there was something in her guarded blue eyes and the way she'd evaded his pursuit into her psyche that told him she usually held a part of herself back in relationships.

Michael wanted it all.

The entire package attracted him, grabbing him in the gut, to the point his attraction to her was almost painful, it went so deep. He wanted to explore every facet, from her gorgeous blonde head to her beautiful unpainted toes. He wanted to know what motivated her, her ambitions and desires. He wanted to know why she'd go along with his story of how they'd met, letting everyone assume she and Michael had been dating. He hoped to hell it was because she was as attracted to him as he was to her.

When Susanna approached, he handed her a glass of wine. She raised her right eyebrow and pursed her lips in a seductive smile before taking a sip. "Trying to prime me?"

He realized she was referring to his earlier comment that she'd taste like a fine merlot and his insides clinched. Even before he'd really gotten to know her, by her selfless actions with her family, he knew the things that mattered to her. Beyond his attraction to her...that was the reason he'd asked her out.

He raised his glass in a "touché" salute. "The evening is still young."

"And the wine bottle is still full," she said with a wink as she raised her glass.

Damn, he wanted this woman with a vengeance. The verbal sparring was almost as good as sex.

Almost.

Michael tilted his head toward a small corner table for two. "Want to grab that table?"

Susan eyed the secluded corner. "You bring the wine and I'm yours." Before she walked away, she gave him a naughty smile.

Picking up the bottle of wine, Michael chuckled. How many double entendres could they exchange in one evening? He damned well planned to find out...along with a lot more about the intriguing woman.

107

Susan sat at the small café table, wine glass in hand as he set the bottle on the table between them.

Her eyebrow arched. "Think one bottle is going to be enough?"

"Depends on if you want to remember our conversation in the morning," he shot back as he sat down and raised his glass in salute.

"Am I going to want to remember it?" Her lips curved upward before she took a long sip.

She was challenging him, and he fucking loved it. "I'll do my best to make sure I'm worth thinking about tomorrow."

"You're doing pretty good so far." A serious look crossed her face and she set her half-full glass on the table. "Tell me, have you always been so focused on what you want in life?"

He topped off her glass and his own before setting the bottle down. "You're referring to Piccoli's?"

When she nodded, he answered honestly. "I've always known I wanted to run my own business. Combining my love for delivering a good meal with entrepreneurship appealed to me on many levels."

"You *like* being the boss." She cast him a knowing smile.

"Calling all the shots has its advantages, but I'm willing to give up control with the right incentive," he said, sliding his gaze suggestively down her body. Pleased with her low laughter, he moved the conversation to her. "What about you? What career have you chosen for yourself?"

She ran her fingers down the stem of her wine glass. "A career that's rewarding and challenging, but one that I've worked very hard to establish and maintain. I work for the PR firm Anderson & Manning."

He could see Susanna pitching to potential clients. Her

open, honest face would be very appealing, while her professional air would instill confidence that she could deliver. She'd already sold him. "You'd fit right in doing that kind of work. It's very satisfying to be at a point in your career where your labors have paid off, isn't it?"

Raising her glass, she nodded. "Here, here...so long as we don't get complacent."

"That word is *not* in my vocabulary."

CR

Susan chuckled at his adamant statement. In the short time she'd known Michael, she would never use the word complacent to describe the man. Intense, hard-working, dedicated, bluntly honest, yes, but never complacent. He was definitely passionate. The man oozed sexual charisma with every heated look, every well-placed touch.

Eyeing him, she asked, "Are you a workaholic, spending every waking hour at your restaurant?"

He shook his head. "No. I love what I do, but I work to live. I don't live to work. Like you, my family is very important to me. I make time for them."

Susan was surprised Michael had picked up on how important family was to her. She nodded. "It's true. I would do just about anything to help out my family if they needed me."

His eyebrow rose. "Like track down the owner of an exclusive restaurant to make sure your brother's rehearsal dinner menu is just right?"

She smiled. That's how he knew. "Exactly." She might put being there for her family pretty high on her priority list, but Michael appeared to have a much better handle on balancing his life. He seemed relaxed and laid back. She'd had to work hard to get where she was in the firm. Only in the last few months had she allowed herself to truly enjoy the fruits of her labor at work.

All work and no play had made her very dull. Michael was a professional, but he was also exciting, spontaneous and so damned sexy. Picking up her glass, she took another drink, enjoying learning about the man behind the seductive veneer and enticing double entendres. "Now that I know how you work, what do you do for fun?"

A devilish grin tilted his lips. "You mean other than pursue you?"

Thoroughly enchanted, she refused to give him an inch—he would take way more than a mile. "Yes, other than that, King of Repartee."

Lifting his nose with a regal air, he spoke as if he were reading his own bio. "His highness has an affinity for roller coasters and collects first edition board games."

Surprised and amused, Susan choked on her wine and quickly set down her glass. She swallowed her gulp of wine, while tears welled. "Roller coasters and board games?"

"When was the last time you rode a roller coaster?" he asked, a curious expression on his face.

She thought back, trying to remember. "Um, probably when I was twelve."

Excitement sparked in his gaze as he leaned on the table. "Remember how free you felt?"

"I remember how my stomach felt. When I lay in bed that night after our trip to the amusement park, I kept feeling that same 'my stomach just met my throat' sensation over and over again. The only thing that stopped it was finally falling into an exhausted sleep."

"It's a thrilling, out of control, free-floating feeling." He sat back in his chair, appreciation reflected in his gaze. "Like being on a first date with a person you've just met."

Susan's gaze collided with his. Every nerve ending in her body jangled to life that he'd equated the exhilarating sensation to being with her. "You're definitely leaving a lasting impression."

Michael flashed a confident grin and held the bottle up. "More wine?"

After he poured more wine for her, he asked, "What do you do to relax?"

"Other than take long hot, baths..." She paused and swirled the wine in her glass, watching the deep red color cling to the sides. "I accept dates from perfect strangers and share a bottle of good merlot with them."

ର

An hour later, Susan and Michael followed the rest of her brother's wedding party out of the bar.

Susan hugged Jason and kissed him on the cheek. Pulling back, she said, "See you at the church, little brother."

Jason smiled. "You okay to drive home?"

Susan laughed and nodded.

"I'll make sure she gets home," Michael said from behind her.

Turning to Michael, she met his gaze. "You plan on following me?"

"Right up to your doorstep."

Her stomach did fluttery flip-flops at the determination in

his tone. She and Michael had exchanged many more double entendres while they'd finished off their bottle of wine. The man was a fantastic, witty conversationalist, not to mention sexy as sin.

Jason looked Michael straight in the eye as he shook his hand. "Thanks for making sure my sister gets home safe. By the way, you're invited to the wedding tomorrow."

Michael grinned, glancing at Susan. "Another date with Susan. How can I refuse?"

"Oh, Susan, do you think you could be at the church an hour earlier tomorrow?" Melanie asked.

Susan groaned inwardly. It was one o'clock in the morning. At this rate, she'd get five hours sleep max before she'd have to be at the church. "Sure, Melanie."

Melanie flashed her a bright smile. "Thanks. See you in the morning."

While Michael escorted her to her vehicle, her body tingled all over when he put his hand at the small of her back. He had her so caught up she barely noticed the cool fall wind. As she slid her key into the lock, his warm breath brushed her neck. "Are you at least going to let me kiss you tonight?"

She jerked her gaze to his. "I...really hadn't thought that far ahead."

"Liar," he said, amusement dancing in his shadowy gaze.

Barely an inch separated them. Time seemed to stand still for several long seconds until he reached around and opened her door for her. "I'll follow you home."

A little disappointed he didn't take advantage of their close proximity, Susan slid into her seat and shut the door. Maybe he wanted to kiss her outside her apartment door?

Her spirits rose at the thought and she started her car,

humming along to the song's upbeat tune on the radio.

She wasn't drunk by a long shot, but the wine had certainly done its job on her inhibitions. All she could think about as she drove home was how Michael's lips would feel against hers, the sensation of his hands on her waist, pulling her close.

By the time she reached her apartment's parking lot, her nerves jangled with pent-up desire. But when she cut her engine, a depressing thought crossed her mind. *I hope Michael can kiss. Damn, I've built it up in my mind so much on the way home the poor man doesn't have a prayer.*

Ironically, she'd never in her life fantasized about a man like this...but then, she'd always made sure to date men she could read. She knew exactly which ones would wait until the third date before trying to kiss her, which ones would shift straight into sex at the end of date number one, and which ones needed their mom's permission to ask her out on date number two. Safe men, staid men...predictable men. She'd dated them all. And had been left numb.

Michael came on full force. He left no doubt he was attracted to her, but the way he listened to her and asked her questions...he set her off-kilter. When he looked at her, his penetrating gaze made her tingle all over. It was as if he already knew her deepest secrets and fears, but he wanted her to share what was buried in her soul.

Michael stood outside her car door and opened it for her. Her skin prickled as he walked beside her toward her high-rise, brick apartment building. Opening the heavy main glass door, he followed her into the lobby.

Susan proceeded to the elevator and pressed the up button. Her insides began to vibrate in aroused overdrive as Michael stepped next to her. She cast a surreptitious glance his way to find the seductive man staring down at her, an inscrutable expression on his face. The elevator arrived and Michael followed her inside.

Once she punched the button for floor nine, she walked to the back of the elevator then turned to face the doors. She gasped when Michael's hand landed on the wall next to her head. He'd moved right into her personal space and stared down at her with his seductive, warm chocolate gaze. Michael's alluring cologne—its scent subtle yet commanding all at once— washed over her. After all the talking they'd done the past few hours, conversation evaporated away while simmering sexual tension boiled to the surface.

As the elevator began to move upward, she stared at his angular jaw. A five o'clock shadow had already begun to form on it. What would it feel like to have his rough stubble against her mouth?

I'm unpredictable, at least tonight, she reminded herself. She licked her lips. "Don't you want to find out if I taste as good as that bottle of merl—"

He cut her off, his lips landing on hers with an intensity that blew her away. Susan's world rocked when he stepped flush against her body, slanting his mouth across hers in a hungry kiss.

He grasped her hips, pulling her even closer, his tongue tangling with hers. Wrapping her arms around his neck, she moaned against him, reveling in his aggressive, dominant mouth pressing against hers. His sexy stubble made her want to kiss him all night long. When Michael's hand cupped her head and tilted it so he could thrust his tongue deeper, her breasts tingled and desire pinged, touching every part of her body like a rubber ball bouncing out of control. She knew sex with him would be just like that...deep, aggressive and unrestrained. Running her tongue alongside his, she gave as good as she got, enjoying their mutual hunger.

When he pressed his erection against her, her lower muscles flexed. Heat spread to her core, radiating in waves of heightened arousal that spread to all the erotic pulse points in her body.

"Ahem!" Someone cleared their throat.

Susan jerked her arms down and peered around Michael's broad shoulders to see her neighbor, Ms. Jenkins, standing in the elevator's open doorway, holding her long-haired, black and brown Chihuahua in her arms.

Embarrassed heat flooded Susan's face at the look of disapproval on the older woman's face. Michael clasped her hand and pulled her off the elevator. "First date," he said with a grin to Ms. Jenkins at the same time the old woman passed them and entered the elevator.

Susan's stomach flip-flopped the entire trip down the hall to her door. She couldn't believe the chemistry between them. It was so intense, so all-consuming of her senses, she'd gotten lost in that kiss to the point she hadn't even felt the elevator stop.

When she unlocked her door, Michael said, "I know you've got to get up early, so I'll say goodnight. See you tomorrow, beautiful."

At a loss for words, she nodded her agreement. The man had totally stunned her with that devastating kiss. Would she survive their next encounter?

She'd opened her door and started to walk inside when Michael spoke, the low register of his voice skidding down her spine. "As for the merlot and tasting you, I wasn't referring to kissing your delectable mouth, Susanna."

His ravenous gaze slowly slid down her body before he

turned and walked away.

༄

The warm summer wind felt good on her bare skin. Susan inhaled the briny air around her and turned her face toward the afternoon sun, soaking up the last few rays before it sank from the sky.

"Come on, slow poke." Michael's deep voice called out above the wind.

Michael stood on the beach, looking up at her. He was wearing sunglasses, worn jeans and a heather gray T-shirt. His sexy grin made her knees weak.

Every. Single. Time.

She waved to him and untied her sweat jacket from around her waist.

Shrugging into it, she zipped the black fleece over her white tank top, then straightened the gathered waist over her fitted, black yoga pants. Sliding her feet out of her white flip-flops, she rolled up her pants legs and collected the thongs in her hand.

She took the wooden stairs two at a time down to the beach. As she walked quickly through the sand, the warm granules squished between her toes, while broken sea shells and dried sponges scattered away from her feet.

"Oooh, hot, hot," she called out, hopping along until she made it to the packed sand.

"Should've left your sandals on," Michael teased her once she reached his side.

She grinned up at him. "I know, but I like the way the sand feels between my toes." Glancing down at her feet, she squished them in the cooler, wet hard sand. "Even if the bottoms of my feet are nice and toasty now."

"I'll massage those burnt toes for you later," he said as he reached out and captured her free hand.

Susan's fingers laced easily with his and she leaned over and kissed him on his jaw, whispering, "Is this before or after our bath?"

As she started to pull away, he quickly turned his head and captured her lips with his. Her heart thumped with happiness and excitement when his sensual mouth claimed hers. His unique, masculine smell surrounded her while the intense, seductive promise behind his possessive kiss seduced her even more.

He slowly pulled his lips away from hers, as if he didn't want their kiss to end, and answered her question in a husky voice, "During."

A pleased shiver ran over her body, despite the warm air. "Promise?" she teased with a grin as the pounding surf rushed up and surrounded their feet. Wet, gray sand sloshed between her toes, chilling them and taking away the heated sting.

"She's bewitched me," he mumbled, then began to walk, tugging her along through the bubbly froth.

"Only just a little." Deep, abiding love filled her. The man had totally stolen her soul as well. Her steps were light and carefree and she fell into a leisurely walking rhythm alongside Michael, their entwined hands swinging between them.

They walked for at least a mile in companionable silence, just enjoying each other's company, the sand on their feet and the sound of the surf in their ears.

The sun had almost set when Michael stopped and pulled her in front of him. Wrapping his arms around her, he molded her back to his chest and faced them toward the ocean.

"*What do you see?*" *he whispered in her ear.*

He sounded so upbeat yet introspective. She smiled and dropped her shoes, hugging his arms with hers. "I see seagulls circling, hoping a tourist will throw them some food, swimmers enjoying the last bit of sun, boats off in the distance coming back from outings. What do you see?"

"*I see a peaceful view I've always wanted to share with someone special.*" *Clasping her hand, he held it in front of them and continued, "I'm looking forward to sharing every single one of them with you."*

Michael made her feel loved and so very cherished. A lump formed in her throat and Susan tried to blink back the tears that filled her eyes, but the wind blew the wet streaks down her cheeks, refusing to let her hold her emotions in.

His grip on her hand tightened, drawing her attention to her left hand lying on top of his.

Her eyes widened in surprise at the beautiful sight before her. The sun shimmered on the facets in her diamond wedding band and engagement ring. The reflection was so brilliant, it blinded her.

Intuitively, she squeezed her eyes shut, then opened them once more.

Susan jerked awake and squinted at the bright sunlight shining directly in her face. Trembling at the surreal emotions still riding high within her, she sat up in bed and let out a shaky breath.

CR

As requested, Susan arrived at the church bright and early. Melanie was true to form, demanding this and that, but through her curt tone and frantic actions, Susan saw most of her future sister-in-law's briskness was due to nerves. When the organ began to play, the bride-to-be's anxiety jumped twenty notches.

Melanie stood in front of the mirror and bit her lip as she adjusted her headpiece over her carefully groomed French twist. As she hitched her strapless, three-thousand-dollar designer wedding gown higher against her breasts, she mumbled, "I hope I don't fall out of this thing."

Susan adjusted her own maroon, strapless silk bridesmaid's gown and said with a wink, "You be careful tossing the bouquet and I'll be careful reaching for it. Deal?"

Melanie giggled. "Deal. Thank you for coming in early and basically being my right arm."

Susan was surprised to hear the young woman thank her...even if she never looked away from her reflection to do so.

She smiled. "You're welcome, Melanie. Soon, you'll be family."

Melanie glanced at her mother, who'd walked up behind her. "Can you believe it? I'll be Melanie Brennon in less than an hour."

The mother-of-the-bride was a tense basket case and had been ever since Susan arrived. *No wonder Melanie wanted me to come in an hour early.* Susan watched Melanie's mother flitter around the dressing room area. Instead of being helpful, her jittery movements only managed to cause additional stress.

Adjusting her daughter's train one last time, her mother stood back. "Hurry up, honey. They're about to cue the wedding march. Hundreds of guests are waiting to see us."

Susan lifted one eyebrow as she glanced at Melanie's mother. Us? Just who was getting married, anyhow?

Patrice Michelle

Picking up the organza shawl that matched her bridesmaid's dress, Susan draped it across her shoulders. "That means I've got to go get ready to walk out with the rest of the bridesmaids." She approached Melanie and put her hand on her shoulder. "Take it one step at a time. I'll see you out there."

Melanie took a deep breath and gave her an unsteady smile.

 началоCR

"The wedding ceremony was wonderful," an older lady said as she walked past, her hand curled around her husband's bent elbow.

Susan must've heard that same comment a hundred times after the wedding and now at the reception. For her, it was a bittersweet occasion. While it *was* a beautiful ceremony, Jason's marriage also marked a new stage in their sibling relationship.

First her parents, then her uncle and now...her baby brother had moved on. It was as if she'd lost everyone she'd ever loved. She knew it was irrational, but she couldn't help feeling the way she did. Jason and she had always shared every holiday together. Now that he was married, he'd probably be spending holidays with his wife's family.

As she'd gazed around the church, her stomach had tensed. All she saw were strangers. Jason's fraternity brothers and their dates had attended the wedding, thankfully filling up the Brennon side of the church pews to full capacity. When the ceremony was over and the bridesmaids had walked down the aisle, Susan's gaze had sought out Michael's.

She didn't know why...but she felt as if she needed a kind of familiar connection among a sea of unfamiliar faces. She

120

spotted Michael sitting in the second pew, and the moment her gaze locked with his steady one, her insides turned warm and her nerves instantly settled.

The wedding guests had moved on to the reception, and Susan now stood next to the open bar, sipping her glass of wine as she took a brief rest. If one more person asked her to smile for the camera, she'd swear her face would crack. Melanie's photographer insisted on taking at least three hundred photos. Since most of the photos were outside and all she had to cover her shoulders was a thin shawl, Susan had sent thanks to Mother Nature for making it a mild fall day.

Scanning the large reception ballroom decked out in black, maroon and silver decorations, she tracked the crowd for any sign of Michael. She hadn't seen him since the wedding, and she'd been at the reception for at least forty-five minutes. Her upbeat mood lowered. Had he only planned to attend the wedding?

The way she was feeling at the moment, shaky and unsettled, combined with the fact Michael's mere presence had calmed her earlier during the wedding ceremony, reminded her of the surreal dream she'd had the night before. She knew she'd dreamed they were married because of her brother's wedding happening the next day, not to mention the wedding was how she'd met Michael, but the way she'd felt about the man in her dream disturbed her a little. Her feelings for him were intense and deeply entrenched. She couldn't possibly have become so attached to him already. *Have fun but stay focused,* she told herself.

Then the group of people standing in front of her parted and her mind shifted from the dream Michael to the very real, very sexy version walking straight toward her, his stride firm and confident. Her gaze drifted over his expensive black tux, noting how well it fit his broad shoulders. The contrast of his

121

Patrice Michelle

white shirt against his olive skin made butterflies flit around in her belly. His dark looks attracted her completely, but it was the intense expression on his face that suddenly made it very hard for her to take a breath.

As soon as he reached her, Michael took her glass and set it on a nearby table. Without a word, he turned and pulled her toward the dance floor.

Susan clutched his hand. "Michael?" she said as she followed behind him at a brisk pace to keep up with his long, commanding strides.

Michael shouldered his way deep into the crowd of people slow dancing. When they reached the center of the dance floor, he wrapped his strong arms around her waist and pulled her body in line with his chest.

Once he began dancing, Michael lowered his head until his lips almost touched hers. Susan's stomach knotted in anticipation. Her breath caught in her throat while she waited for him to move that last quarter inch. Instead, he kissed her jaw and spoke next to her ear.

"All I thought about last night was you."

Every nerve ending skittered to attention. She bit her lower lip.

"And do you know why?"

She shook her head at his question and waited for his answer.

"Because your scent was all over me. On my clothes, on my hands. You smell like sheer temptation. Intoxicating and alluring."

Susan swallowed and mentally vowed to buy out the department store's supply of her perfume. The man truly left her speechless. She took a steadying breath. "My scent kept you awake?"

When his lips grazed her ear lobe, she hoped he'd nip at the sensitive skin. Her breasts swelled and her nipples tightened in expectation.

"Mm hm. I kept trying to figure out what you'd smell like once you're flushed from arousal, and I just couldn't conjure the scent." His hands slid under her shawl, touching her bare back. "I figure I'll just have to find out first-hand."

His warm fingers brushing against her skin caused a slow burn to spread across her back. Susan dug her own fingers into his shoulder while her other hand clasped the material on the back of his tux jacket.

"You left me with very diverting thoughts yourself last night," she whispered.

This time he kissed the spot behind her ear. "Good. I'm glad to know I wasn't alone in my consuming thoughts while I lay in bed."

The mental image of Michael sprawled out across his bed thinking of her made a shiver of awareness course through her.

The slow song ended and the mother-of-the-bride walked up to the mike. "If I could have all the bridesmaids up at the front, please."

Susan cast Michael an apologetic look. "I'm afraid it'll probably be like this the rest of the evening."

He kissed her hand. "It's okay. I have some things I need to take care of anyway."

He was leaving? Her excitement tanked along with her quickened pulse rate.

"After the reception, go home and take a nap. You have a date tonight."

"I do?" She lifted her eyebrow in surprise, her heart

tripping.

A devilish grin spread across his face. "You do. We're going to enjoy some more merlot together."

"Merlot?" Her thoughts immediately reverted to the comment he'd left her with last night, and her body began to quiver deep inside.

He nodded. "Come by Piccoli's at ten o'clock."

She called out her agreement as two bridesmaids swept her away toward the front of the reception room.

ରେ

Susan stood in front of Piccoli's staring at the black granite sign with its gold lettering. *What a difference a couple days make*, she thought as a plethora of carnal scenarios with Michael and a bottle of merlot bounced around in her mind. She felt like a very different person from the woman who'd stood staring at this same sign just a few days ago.

Once she'd seen her little brother drive away with his new bride, she'd done as Michael suggested and taken a much needed long nap that afternoon. Then she'd spent the rest of her waking moments looking forward to her evening with Michael. Once she'd tugged her black jacket closer around her royal blue silk blouse, she smoothed her hands over the black skirt that stopped a couple inches above her knees.

Opting for a skimpy black bra and matching underwear underneath her clothes made her feel ready for anything. An amused smile tugged on her lips as she remembered how her mom had always said, "You should wear your best underwear at all times, dear. You never know when you'll be in an accident."

I don't plan on being in an accident tonight, but this man is certainly dangerous enough to warrant caution. She chuckled inwardly as she pulled on the thick handle and opened the door.

"Good evening, Ms. Brennon." A dark-haired man in his mid-twenties approached and bowed formally as she entered the empty restaurant.

At her quizzical look, he smiled. "Michael told me to expect you. I'm Stephan. Let me take your jacket and purse for you."

After she shrugged out of her jacket and handed him her purse, Susan waited for him to hang them in a closet off the entryway.

Stephan closed the closet door and turned back to her with a pleasant smile. Handing her a glass of merlot he had sitting on the host's stand, he said, "Michael asks that you meet him in the cellar."

"The cellar?"

He nodded and pointed toward a door in the back of the restaurant. "Go through that door and take the stairs down."

When he opened the door and started out the entrance she'd just come in, Susan asked, "You're leaving?"

Stephan smiled at her, his olive-toned complexion reminding her of Michael's. "Piccoli's is closed for the evening. Have a great night."

While Stephan locked the outer door, she thought it interesting that Michael would entrust an employee with the key to his restaurant. Then Michael's story about the man who'd believed in him and backed him financially came to her. *Trust had to start somewhere. Michael knew that better than anyone.* She walked toward the back of the restaurant, excitement skidding up her spine.

Her heels clicked on the cement stairs as she made her way down to the cellar. Once she'd reached the floor, she gasped at the rows and rows of bottles all lined up neatly on racks of shelves twenty feet deep to her left. To her right, a long wooden table stood next to the wall. The soft, subdued lighting gave the room a very quiet feel...almost as if she had to keep her voice down so the wine would continue to age properly.

The wine cellar was a good ten degrees cooler than the main floor. The coolness felt good against her skin as she set her glass on a granite shelf above the table and began to walk down one of the long aisles, following the dim track lighting on the floor.

Merlots, Chiantis, Cabernets, Rieslings, Pinot Grigios and Chardonnays...you name it, Piccoli's had it, from the very high-end range to midlevel price points.

Impressive.

But where was Piccoli's intriguing owner? "Michael?"

As soon as she spoke, the room went completely dark. Susan gasped. Her heart began to hammer. Surely Michael was behind this. Trying to remain calm, she was afraid to reach out and attempt to feel her way back down the aisle. She could see herself knocking down a couple of the three-hundred-dollar bottles of wine on her way up the aisle in "blind" mode.

But Susan was never one to stand still in life. The lights at her feet put off a very low glow, but they did provide a path. She started to turn back when someone wrapped his hands around her waist from behind.

Fear gripped her throat, fisting it tight. Her scream came out in a garbled mewl at the same time Michael whispered against her ear. "Shhh. It's just me."

Chapter Three

Her pulse rushed double time from the spike of fear and Michael's close proximity. Clutching his hand at her waist, she let her back melt against his hard chest.

"Are you trying to give me a heart atta—" she started to ask.

But Michael's next words cut her off. "Don't you want to know how I found you in the dark?"

She nodded then realized he might be able to see her feet, but he couldn't see her face. "Yes."

Michael's fingers flexed around her waist, and he took a deep breath next to her neck. "I followed your scent."

Before she could respond, he splayed his fingers across her ribcage and continued. "When one of the senses is taken away, the others will kick in, compensating for the loss."

"What other senses kicked in?" she asked with a sigh of pleasure when his lips trailed down the side of her throat.

He nipped at her neck. "My sense of smell is very keen, but it's my sense of taste I want to explore in intimate detail with you."

Susan's sex began to throb in pent-up arousal at his seductive words.

She raised her hands behind her to loop them around his

neck, pulling him closer. Sliding her fingers upward into his thick hair, she agreed. "I'd like to learn more about your senses, too."

His fingers moved to the buttons on her blouse. As he began to unbutton the silk material with slow movements, he kissed her jaw. "The cellar was the perfect place to bring you for this tasting."

She closed her eyes at the things this man made her feel. She'd never felt so achingly desperate to have a man touch her like she did this one.

"Want to know why?" Michael asked as the first button gave way.

"Why?"

"Because smell and taste are two of the most important senses in wine tasting." He finished unbuttoning her blouse and started to trail his fingers up her waist and across her ribcage toward her breasts.

"Do you...um...offer...wine tastings down here?" She opened her eyes and wrangled out her question between tantalizing sensations rippling through her body. Soon her brain wouldn't be able to perform cognizant, upper-level thinking. Well, one thought would continue to run crazily through her mind. *He's driving me insane with his teasing touches.*

"Yes, Piccoli's offers wine tastings, but not the kind we're about to embark on," he purred next to her ear.

"Oh good. I've always liked private lessons. I usually retain a lot more that way."

His low chuckle reverberated against her back. She liked Michael, liked the way he made her feel and how easily he caused her inhibitions to simply disappear. Susan let out a low moan when he cupped her breasts through her lacy bra.

"I'll be sure to take my time then. I wouldn't want you to forget a thing about tonight." He pressed his erection against her backside as he ran his thumbs along her nipples. His touch caused them to harden even more.

"Not too much time," she breathed out with a laugh. Her legs were already turning to rubber and her sex pulsed painfully at his suggestive words. Susan covered his hand with hers and led his fingers to the hook between her breasts that held the scraps of her bra together.

While Michael unhooked her bra, he slid his other hand up her arm around his neck and laced his fingers with hers. His breathing increased when his warm fingers clasped her breast. Her heart was too busy hammering at record speeds for her to say a word. Instead, her stomach fluttered as he pulled her hand from around his neck and moved it between them where he wrapped her fingers around his cock.

Emboldened by his need to feel her touch, Susan didn't let the fact she was standing with her back to him slow their intimacy. She flattened her palm against the hard ridge of flesh pressing against her buttocks then curled her fingers around his erection, sliding them lower to include every part of him.

Michael groaned against her neck. He nibbled at the soft flesh and his hips moved forward, locking her hand between his body and hers. "You make me crave every part of you. I've never ached to taste a woman as much as I do you."

"Then what's stopping you?" she asked, turning her head sideways and tilting her face toward his.

"I wanted to take this slow."

She felt the heat of his mouth right above hers, smelled his masculine cologne and the scent of merlot on his breath. Her skin prickled.

"I'm a breath away. We can take it slow another night." She

hoped she sounded sultry and not desperate, but the truth was...she desperately wanted to experience Michael's body aligned with hers, to feel his heart pound against her chest and know he was just as affected as she was.

As if her permission was all he needed, Michael turned her to face him. His hands slid up her back and his fingers branded her skin with his heat. His lips collided with hers, hitting the corner of her mouth.

She smiled and moved her head slightly, assuming he'd missed his target. But when Michael's mouth connected with the other corner of her lips, she realized his slow, teasing seduction was very purposeful.

"I'm right here," she encouraged in a whisper.

His fingers massaged her upper back and he pulled her close until her nipples brushed against his dress shirt. One of the buttons rubbed a sensitive tip, making her want to scream in frustration, while his mouth forged a hot path up her jaw.

"When I kiss you this time, I won't stop until you're begging me to."

"Is that a promise?" She really hoped it was.

"I want to hear you panting, to know what you smell like when you're fully aroused and sweaty from sex. I don't want to fantasize any longer."

Susan couldn't help but shiver at his intimate words. That was definitely a promise! Her exposed skin pebbled in excitement, yet heat spread throughout her body like fireworks flying in a zillion directions.

"Then you'd better kiss me. Chill bumps don't go with sweat."

His fingers slid across her back, touching her raised skin as if he wanted proof she spoke the truth. When his hand lowered and he palmed her hip in a tight hold, she sensed the sexual tension building within him and realized he was just as caught up in the moment as she was.

Susan tilted her head to give him better access to her mouth and waited, her breath caught in her throat.

Michael's lips covered hers and desire shot straight through her chest then down between her thighs. She adored how his mouth applied just the right amount of pressure to let her know he wanted more.

Moving her hands up his shoulders, she slid them around his neck. She teased the tip of his tongue with hers. Michael groaned and ran his tongue alongside hers in a slow, sensual glide. She kissed him then sucked on his tongue.

He grunted and his hands slid lower. Before she knew it, his hands were cupping her ass as he lifted her against him.

Susan let out a surprised gasp then smiled her approval that he'd taken their foreplay to a much closer level. She clung to him, glad her shorter skirt allowed her to wrap her legs around his trim hips. When she locked herself against him, finally, she felt it—his heart slamming against his chest, just like hers. Her electric attraction to Michael might jumpstart her pulse, but from the moment they'd met, something about him felt comforting and familiar. He'd never felt like a stranger to her.

Maybe because he'd ensconced himself in her life at such a rapid pace she didn't have a chance to erect the normal walls she did around herself. This man left her breathless, feeling a bit out of control...as if she were constantly trying to catch up. It was an exhilarating and unique feeling...one she planned to indulge in tonight.

Michael trailed kisses down her neck as he turned and walked toward the entrance of the cellar. Sparks splintered through her at his possessive hold on her body. Susan relished every minute of his burning kisses and thanked the stars above he knew his way around the cellar in the dim light.

When he set her down on a hard surface, the track lighting glowed on the bottom stair behind him. She realized he'd lowered her to the wooden table she'd seen when she'd entered the cellar earlier.

Michael stood between her legs as she tugged his shirt out of his pants and fumbled with the buttons down its front.

Soft lighting suddenly came on above them and she blinked in surprise until her eyes adjusted to the change. They came into focus and she stared at Michael's bare chest as he lowered his hand from the light switch on the wall. God, the man had a beautiful body. A light coating of dark hair sprinkled across his muscular pectorals before it thinned into an inviting line that disappeared past his toned stomach and waistline of his dress pants.

She couldn't resist touching the hard chest in front of her. When her fingers connected with his skin, his body tensed.

Afraid she'd done something wrong, Susan jerked her gaze to his.

It was one thing to feel Michael's passion, but the sensual look in his bedroom eyes as he stared at her took her breath away. His heated gaze slowly lowered to devour her breasts and her puckered nipples.

Feeling more confident, Susan laid her hands on the table behind her. She arched her back and gave him a seductive smile. "Are you going to sample them or just stare at them?"

Michael raised his eyebrows at her challenging comment. A wicked smile tugged at his lips as he retrieved the glass of wine that sat on the shelf next to her. The look on his face told her he had plans for that wine. The devil! He'd planned this breathtaking seduction...and she thrilled in every minute of it.

He took a sip and set the glass back where he found it. Placing his hands on the table on either side of her, he drew close, but didn't touch her. They stared at each other, tension arcing between them.

Susan took an unsteady inhale, unsure what to do or say next. Michael surprised her when he lowered his head and clamped his mouth around her nipple. The dual sensation of his warm mouth cooled by the wine only fueled her libido. She gasped at the electricity that zinged through her. He didn't ease her into it...he sucked hard and with immediacy as if he couldn't get enough of her.

Susan's sex pulsed at the pressure he applied and she couldn't help the moan of sheer pleasure that escaped when he nipped at the hard tip. Without a second thought, she lifted her hands and cupped the back of his head, pulling him closer.

Michael placed his hands on her bare thighs underneath her skirt. His fingers flexed on the muscles as if he wanted to move his hands higher.

Susan opened her legs wider to let him know she was more than willing to accommodate his wishes.

He lifted his head and met her gaze, his chocolate brown eyes churning with varied emotions, desire front and center. An unspoken, seductive communication passed between them as his fingers moved to the button on the side of her short, wraparound skirt. She normally didn't jump into intimacies like this, usually reserving them for long-standing relationships, but with Michael the connection felt so right...more than with any other man. Her stomach fluttered when he freed the button and pulled her skirt open, revealing her sexy black panties underneath.

She set her hands down on the table and let her head fall

back, silently inviting him to touch her, to move his hands higher.

When she felt his heated breath a second before his mouth came in contact with her sex through her underwear, Susan gasped and lowered her gaze to his dark head. Her core clenched at his incredibly sexy, intimate kiss.

She throbbed painfully, surprised she wanted to demand more when she'd expected so much less.

Michael's hands moved to her rear as he kissed her again. This time, he grasped her ass and his kiss was harder yet slower, as if he couldn't resist lingering.

She threaded her fingers in his thick hair and was taken aback when he shuddered and groaned as he ran his tongue along her damp underwear. His shoulders tensed and he moved to plant a kiss on her belly before he laid his forehead against the smooth skin. "I've barely tasted you and I'm ready to explode," he rasped, his breathing sounding harsher.

He wasn't the only one. She scooted back a little on the table then lay down fully on the surface, panting out, "The ties."

Michael lifted her ankles and placed her heels on the edge of the table. His probing gaze locked with hers as he reached for the ties on her bikini underwear and tugged them both open in one swift pull. Then he lowered his head once more and kissed the underwear out of his way until her wet entrance was fully exposed.

It wasn't just his mouth moving toward her sex that had Susan so caught up in the intense man. It was the way he slid his hands down her thighs and gently pressed them apart as if he revered everything about her that knocked her for a loop.

Her throat closed when she glanced down and faced the reality of his tanned hands against her fair skin. When she'd fantasized about him touching her, she hadn't thought it would

134

be such an enchanting scenario. She realized he'd wanted this moment to be about her, yet he'd planned it in such a way to make it about him as well. The thought melted her all over.

His tongue slid up her entrance, aggressive and determined, then his mouth fully connected with her body. Susan's heart rate skyrocketed. She cried out in sheer bliss while her back arched of its own accord. He had her. In so many ways, the man had her!

She closed her eyes and reveled in what it felt like to be in the arms of a man who knew how to please a woman on a spontaneous level. All her past relationships had always been carefully planned dates, and carefully planned sex was always the result. Her time with Michael was nothing like she'd ever experienced, which made her wonder why the hell she'd waited so long to say "yes". She knew why—it had to be the right kind of man. Michael was her right kind of man.

Her body tensed as he ran his tongue over every spot, exploring every crease and crevice, tasting her juices thoroughly. She wasn't far from climaxing. He was slowly making his way toward her sensitive bud and the anticipation was killing her. She felt on the verge, ready to leap at any moment.

"I want you to wait for me."

Michael's comment made her pause in tense, sexual frustration. Had she been waiting for him emotionally, too? Nah. It was true this man made her feel free, but what they had was just a fling. Anything more would only lead to heartache later. Every time she'd formed strong attachments in her past she'd been left behind—first her parents, then her uncle and now her little brother was moving on.

Michael was like a strong wind and she was the chimes hanging in the air...unable to resist reacting to his presence moving all around her, making her play a unique melody just for him. The way she felt so free around him, so in tune, like she did in her dream, scared her. As his warm hands trailed with intimate surety over her skin, her entire body trembled. She was afraid she could really learn to care deeply for this man.

That scared her.

She thrilled in their strong attraction and sexual connection, but she resolved to keep her emotions closely guarded while spending time with this irresistible Italian.

The sensation of his finger sliding deep inside her was more than she could handle. She began to shake, holding back from climaxing. Heat spread all over her while her breathing increased to a steady pant. Her skin began to glisten. "I—I can't wait."

"I love how responsive you are." Another finger joined the first. He thrust then turned his fingers upward toward her belly, his knuckles brushing her sensitive skin. "You don't have to wait any more," he said right before he pressed on her hot spot deep inside. At the same time he captured her nub with his lips and sucked on the highly sensitized tip.

Susan screamed and rocked her hips against him as she came. Rippling waves of pleasurable sensations scattered through her. Her skin flushed hot then cold as every crest rushed through her. She clenched her convulsing walls around his fingers, wanting to hold on to the body-rocking moment as long as she could. Just when she thought she was done, Michael began to thrust his fingers deeper, touching every delicate part of her as he laved at her sex once more.

Intense pleasure built in an impending storm once more within her. She climaxed again, moaning at the all-encompassing tremors. She'd barely caught her breath from the second orgasm when his mouth connected with her over-sensitized clit, obviously ready for another round.

She clamped her thighs around his head and begged, "Please, Michael. Don't you want to—"

"More than anything." He withdrew his fingers from her body and quickly lifted his head, his expression full of sexual frustration. She watched in fascination as he slid the two damp fingers inside his mouth. While he savored her taste, his eyes, dark with arousal, locked with hers for several electrifying seconds, snatching her ability to move, let alone speak.

CR

Michael watched Susan's rapt expression and her beautiful eyes lower to his fingers as he sucked her juices from them. Damn, she made him hard as a fucking metal pole! The sensation of her body eagerly clasping his fingers with an unyielding, never-let-him-go grip made his cock throb and his balls ache for release.

In all his thirty-five years, oral sex with a woman had never been this erotic and strangely fulfilling in a ball-busting kind of way. He'd wanted to climb up on the table, unzip his pants and slam his cock deep inside her warm, wet body until they both groaned in sexual fulfillment.

Yet he was glad he'd stuck to his convictions. The look in her eyes, the total amazement at his enjoyment in her unique flavor and the act of making her come while holding back his own pleasure, helped him get a handle on his sexual needs. No woman made him this selfless. He'd found the entire sexual experience with Susan an unexpected aphrodisiac. But he also wanted to make sure their relationship went deeper than just their mutual attraction for each other.

Patrice Michelle

The way she held back some of her moans told him she was still fighting herself around him. He didn't want bits and pieces of her...he wanted the whole uncensored, uninhibited package, because he knew once they finally had sex, it'd be days before he let her up for air.

Pulling his fingers from his mouth, he grasped her hands and helped her to a sitting position. "I want you more than you'll ever know, but not tonight."

Shock crossed her expressive face. "What!"

Chapter Four

A muscle ticced in Michael's jaw as he hooked her bra back in place. When his fingers moved to button her shirt, Susan grasped his hands, her stomach tensing.

"What's wrong?"

He finished his task and the look of restrained desire in his gaze made a hard knot fist in her throat.

Confusion caused her belly to ache. "I can see in your eyes you want to continue...but, I don't understand. Talk to me, Michael."

He turned his hands over and captured hers. Raising her fingers to his mouth, he brushed his lips over her knuckles before he spoke. "I do plan to talk to you, but not here."

She raised an eyebrow. "Where, then?"

"When I get you back to your apartment."

Still perplexed by his comment, Susan let out a relieved breath to know he wasn't planning on leaving her with things unfinished between them.

Once Michael helped her down from the table, she held her hand out for her underwear. He gave her a naughty smile and shook his head as he shoved her panties in his front pants pocket.

She chuckled as she retrieved her skirt from the table and

wrapped it around her waist.

After she'd buttoned it, his smile widened. "No one will know you're naked under there but me."

"I will," she snorted as she followed him out of the cellar.

ભ

The elevator was crowded when Michael and Susan got on. Michael moved them to the left side and wrapped his arms around her waist. He settled her back against his chest as the elevator door closed.

As they headed up, the way she felt in his arms, secure, like she'd be there forever, reminded her of her dream. She felt too close, too connected to this man already. Michael's selfless act of giving her oral sex without expecting anything in return really threw her. Maybe it was just *her* feeling this way. She'd better set the "light-hearted relationship" expectation early on. Turning her head, she whispered in his ear, "Have you ever had sex in public?"

His heart rate ramped up, thudding in rapid beats against her back. She grasped his hand around her waist and tilted her head to the side to hear his whispered answer. "Yes." Her breasts tingled and her core clenched in sheer excitement. The man was so sexually adventurous. She'd never done anything so daring.

Susan moved even closer to his hard frame and shivered deep inside when she felt his erection press against her rear and lower back.

Michael's hands tightened around her waist. He kissed the curve of her ear. "You're killing me, especially since I know you're naked underneath this skirt."

She couldn't help the pleased grin that crossed her face. Her arousal escalated and she purposefully ground her butt against his erection.

His low growl rumbled against her back at the same time the elevator stopped.

Three people got off and six got on.

Susan was forced to align the rest of her body against Michael to make room for the additional passengers. She was so close she felt the entire outline of his cock imprinting itself on her ass. Sexual tension roared within her, making her nipples ache to be tweaked and her sex wet for his kisses and the sensation of his cock stretching her as he thrust deep.

He groaned against her neck and his warm breath bathed her skin, his tone a sexy rasp. "Since I can't do anything about this torture, I'll just tell you what I *want* to do to you."

Her libido vaulted to the ceiling. She encouraged him in a low, excited voice. "Do tell."

His mouth grazed the curve of her ear. "I know sliding inside you will be like finding heaven. I can't wait to feel you taking every inch, to feel your warm body soaking me. I'm going to enjoy every damned thrust drowning in your sweet wetness, Susanna."

His erection slid back and forth against her rear and his erotic words made her feel all woozy deep inside. Susan's breathing increased while her face flooded with the blush of unadulterated arousal.

She closed her eyes and rocked her hips against him, a counter to his relentless pressure against her backside.

When Michael's hands suddenly clamped down on her hips, ceasing her movements, Susan opened her eyes to see Ms. Jenkins' wide-eyed stare locked on his firm hold on her hips. Apparently the elevator had stopped and everyone else had exited except the older lady. Her wrinkled hands clutched her shaking pooch closer to her chest and her condemning crystal blue eyes locked with Susan's.

Embarrassed heat flooded Susan's cheeks, making her feel faint.

Michael took it all in stride. He kissed Susan on the cheek and said, "Second date," to Ms. Jenkins before he walked out of the elevator, tugging Susan along.

Michael made her feel so free, Susan's mortification quickly turned to humor. As she stood in front of her apartment door, she had to hold back her laughter at the memory of the holier-than-thou expression on her neighbor's face.

The older lady cast a disapproving "harrumph" when she passed them, shuffling her way down the hall toward her own apartment door in her fluffy, baby-pink bedroom slippers.

Susan clamped one hand over her mouth to keep from laughing out loud, while she slid her key into the lock and turned the knob to open her door.

Before she could walk inside, Michael cupped his hand around her neck and turned her back toward him, pulling her against his chest.

His mouth covered hers in a heated kiss that stole the words she'd been forming to invite him in.

When her tongue brushed against his, he thrust his against hers once, twice, then a third time before he broke their kiss. The hungry look in his shadowed gaze made her feel like she was the sexiest woman who had ever existed.

Then he released his hold and stepped back, an apologetic expression on his face, and she realized he was going to leave. Her heart jerked at the letdown. She clasped his arm, halting any further retreat. "I thought we were going to talk."

Michael closed his eyes for a brief second and she noted the tension in his face at the same time his fingers gripped hers. "There's nothing I would love to do more than walk inside your apartment with you, but I plan to keep my promise to talk to you."

"And how are you going to do that out here?"

Without a word Michael pulled a cell phone out of his jacket pocket and dialed a number.

The telephone in her apartment started to ring. Susan cast him a confused look. "You have my phone number in your cell phone?" It was entirely possible. Her number was listed in the phonebook.

"Your phone's ringing. I think you'd better answer it." He put his cell phone up to his ear and gave her an encouraging smile before he walked away.

She wasn't sure what Michael's plans were, but the incessant ringing of her phone drew her like Pavlov's dog...*must answer*. She walked inside, shut the door and picked up her cordless handset from the end table next to her couch.

Pushing the talk button, she put the phone to her ear. "Hey."

"Better lock your door, love."

Susan let out a sigh at the sound of his bone-melting baritone. If she couldn't have him with her, at least she could listen to his voice. She kicked off her shoes and walked over to slide the deadbolt on her door.

"Michael, I don't understand..."

"Did you know I have five brothers?"

Susan sank onto her overstuffed, toffee-colored couch, kicked the decorative navy blue pillows out of her way and curled her feet underneath her. He had her attention. "No, I didn't. Knowing what life was like with *one* brother...let's just say I feel for your poor mother. And where do you fall in the litter?"

His low chuckle made her stomach flip-flop.

"I'm the oldest."

She laughed. "Ah ha. I knew it!"

"I love the way you laugh."

Her laughter slowed and silence came across the line for several seconds.

"The truth is...I want you more than I've wanted another woman, Susanna. You make me ache. I knew if I followed you inside your apartment, we'd do very little talking."

Her lower muscles flexed at the seductive purr in his tone.

"I want to get to know your mind just as much as your body."

His serious words made her appreciate him even more. Did that mean what she thought it meant? That Michael was slowing things down and taking the time to get to know her because he wanted something more? The thought both scared and excited her.

She settled back on the couch, her spirits rising. "You're a very astute man. Tell me about your brothers. Are they as tempting as you?"

His car door closed and the sound of an engine starting came across the line.

"As far as you're concerned, my brothers don't hold a candle to me."

She shook her head at his typical male posturing. "You know what I meant."

The rev of his engine sounded in the background as if he'd just pulled into traffic. "Jonathan's the brainy one, Sean's the handy man, Joshua's the wanderer, Keith's the artsy type and Stephan's the youngest and the most like me. You met him tonight."

She did? Susan frowned for a brief second, and then the picture of the dark-haired man who'd closed up Piccoli's popped into her mind. "Is Stephan the young man who took my coat and handed me the glass of wine tonight?"

"He is. As soon as he's done with school, he wants to open his own restaurant."

"And how do you feel about having a brother as a competitor?" she asked.

Michael laughed. "He won't know anything I haven't taught him. Now, give him five years and I'll be a bit concerned. But hopefully by then I'll have convinced him to open another Piccoli's across town."

She loved hearing the pride in Michael's voice when he spoke of his brother. "Sounds like you have a stake in his success."

"In a way, I do. Ten years ago, while my mother went through chemotherapy for cancer, I knew my dad needed to focus on her. I took over raising Stephan until my mom was fully recovered. Ever since then my little brother and I have had a special bond."

While he told her a few amusing stories about Stephan as a teenager and having to have "the talk" with him about the proper use of condoms, she walked into her bedroom, turned on the bedside lamp and lay down on her bed.

After Michael finished, Susan laughed and felt an even deeper connection to him due to their similar circumstances. "I know what you mean. Even though I'm only four years older than Jason, for the longest time he and I had more of a mother/son relationship. Only in the past few years have we been able to talk on the same level. Now it's a mostly sister/brother relationship."

"Ahh, I thought I heard Jason mention that you'd raised him. What happened to your parents?"

Her heart constricted. Even after so long, she still missed them. "My parents died in a car accident twelve years ago. I've been Jason's mom, confidant, mentor, sister, you name it, ever since."

His car door slammed in the background. He must've made it home. "I knew there was something I admired about you. I saw your closeness to Jason. He's very protective over you."

"He is?" She was surprised by his comment. It had always felt the other way around.

"He thanked me for making sure you got home safe, remember?"

"He was just being polite," she scoffed.

"No, you didn't see the look in his eyes or feel how hard he squeezed my hand. His expression and rock-solid grip held quite an interesting challenge that basically said, 'I'll kick your ass if you screw with my sister'."

"And I'll kick your ass if you don't," she replied with a grin at Michael's interpretation. Apparently Jason really *had* grown up under her nose.

His low chuckle came across with seductive undertones. "I love a woman who's not afraid to tell me what she wants."

Emboldened by the fact he'd moved their conversation to sexual banter, Susan asked, "You still have my underwear, which means I'm lying here in my bed with—"

"Nothing covering that sweet body of yours," he finished for her. "What do you sleep in? A T-shirt, frilly lingerie or nothing at all?"

Her breasts tingled at his intimate question. She bent her knees and dug her toes into the bed's soft comforter. "I thought you said you wanted to get to know me?" she teased as she ran her fingers down her bare thigh, pulling her skirt back.

"I am getting to know you...on a *very* personal level. Tell me," he urged.

"I usually sleep in a T-shirt. Soooo sex-ay," she said in a dry tone.

"It is if you're wearing *my* T-shirt and nothing else." He exhaled as if he were sitting down or stretching. "I'm now lying on my own bed with this sexy scrap of black underwear in my hand to remind me of your naked state."

His comment left her completely breathless. "And what *would* you do if I was lying there beside you wearing your T-shirt and nothing else?" Her fingers moved lightly along her inner thigh as she waited for his response.

CR

Michael's cock grew hard with the knowledge she was open to verbal foreplay. He couldn't believe in all his thirty-five years he'd never had phone sex. Susan made it one of the most enticing "nevers" he looked forward to remedying.

"I'd slide my fingertips back and forth across your nipples until they hardened, begging me to suck them."

"And then what?" she asked in a breathless voice.

Michael smiled as he unbuttoned his pants and unzipped his zipper. "Are you hot, Susanna?"

"Mm hm, and wet. What would you do next?" she encouraged.

He immediately conjured a mental picture of her—blonde

hair spread out from her beautiful face and lying across his dark blue sheets. Her pink sex would be swollen and glistening. She'd be ready, eager and so damned reactive to his touch...just like she was earlier. His brain left the room and his body reacted, skin tingling with tiny pinpricks as his balls tightened painfully. If he didn't come soon, he'd spontaneously explode.

"I'd slip my hand under your shirt and spread my fingers across your belly while I captured your nipple in my mouth. I'd want to hear that breathy little moan you make when you want more, so I'd suck hard, T-shirt and all until you came off the bed, begging me to remove the rest of your clothes."

"That's exactly what I'd do," she said, her mewling soft sigh yanking a physical response from him like the gentle brush of her fingers across his aching erection.

Michael slid his hand down into his underwear and gripped his cock. Closing his eyes, he fought the need to come...all brought on by his strong imagination and the sound of her hitched breath. "Imagine me sliding my fingers down your thigh, enjoying the feel of your soft skin."

"Mmmmm," was the only response he got. He smiled as he pumped his hand up and down his cock.

"When you finally touch me, you'll feel just how wet I am, how warm and tight," she said. "I push your pants down, not even bothering to get them all the way off you before I grab your erection and lead you to me...I want you that much."

Her breathing had changed, along with the "what they'd do" scenario. She was with him real-time. He felt the heat and need in her voice. He knew she was sliding her fingers inside her channel, and at the erotic realization he closed his eyes for a brief second. "I'm sliding inside you, Susanna. What do you do?"

"I—I'm so close. You feel so good. You press against me and

I welcome the fullness of your weight on me. You're heavy and hard as you move inside me. I want to scream, but instead..." she paused and sighed before finishing in a vixen's tone, "I wrap my legs around your waist and dig my nails deep into your shoulders."

Michael's heart thumped hard at the provocative scenario she painted. He loved this give and take. His turn. "I bury my nose in your throat and hair, inhaling your scent as I drive inside you. I thrust hard and deep, because I know with you...I'll never get enough." His body jerked at the thought of the acts behind his words, things he really wanted to do with her. He groaned. "I want to stay buried as far as I can get. Forever."

Susan didn't speak, but he heard her staccato pants. As much as he wanted to make himself come, he needed to hear the sounds of her climaxing even more, so he gave her what she needed. "I rock into you and grind my hips against yours until you scream—"

"Yes, God...yes!" she answered, interrupting him, her breathing expelling in heavy gusts. Michael's pulse rushed in his ears and his cock turned to smooth granite in his hand. He pumped harder, so on edge he ground his teeth to keep from yelling out.

When she sighed, he managed to continue in an unaffected tone, "I felt your spasms lock me in a vise hold, sweetheart. I'd want that sensation to go on forever...for both of us."

"Then you'd better let go, Michael. You're tense and you need a release. You've held back long enough. I'm warm and eager and moving just right so you tap against the hottest, wettest spots deep inside me. That's the most sensitive part, isn't it? The tip of your cock."

Michael held back the growl that threatened to release from

his throat as he slid his hand all the way down his erection and back up, cupping the tip of his cock. She was right, of course.

"Imagine I'm running my tongue all around the tip, right before I take all of you deep down my throat. And then I suck...long and hard."

Her explicit words, describing in intimate detail an act he would love to watch her perform, sent him over the edge. Michael's body jerked as he came, his hips moving in hard punches toward the ceiling then slamming back on the bed. He'd denied himself too long and the pent-up sexual frustration made his orgasm both pleasurable and painful all at once.

When a low groan erupted from him, her sexy voice brought him back down to earth as his heart pounded like a jackhammer. "You know the great thing about this kind of sex?"

"What's that?"

"Very little clean up and no condom to dispose of."

"Speak for yourself," he said, dreading the job. Her light-hearted laugh at his dry response made his lips tug upward in a broad smile.

As her laughter died down, silence came across the line. The quiet simmered just under the surface, their building attraction like a thin bed sheet between them, letting them feel everything, but still keeping them apart.

Susan exhaled in a soft sigh. "Well, I'd better get some sleep. I have a plane to catch tomorrow morning."

Michael's gut tensed. He'd been planning to ask her to go out to dinner tomorrow night. "Where are you going?"

"I'm taking a business trip to Virginia."

"When will you get back?"

"I'll be back Wednesday night. You going to miss me?" she teased.

"Yes, I will." He was surprised how disappointed he was to learn she'd be gone for three days.

"Good."

Damn if the pleased tone in her voice didn't arouse him all over again.

Chapter Five

"There's a Mr. Piccoli on line two for you."

"Thanks, Callie." Susan picked up the phone and punched the button for line two. As anticipation thrummed, making her skin pebble, she tried to sound casual. "Hey, Michael."

"You didn't say that the name of your firm was Anderson, Manning & Brennon."

She smiled at the deep respect that laced his chiding. "The third name was just added a couple months ago."

"Bravo to you, Susanna. I have a project I've got to do. Would you like to come along this evening?"

She stood and leaned against her desk to face the huge picture window behind her chair. Smiling at the secret tone in Michael's voice, she pressed the telephone receiver closer to her ear. "How should I dress?"

"Wear black."

The way he said "black" sounded clandestine and naughty. "Definitely. Where do you want me to meet you?"

"I'll pick you up at your apartment at six. We'll go to dinner first."

And the naughty part later. "Sounds like a plan. See you then."

She started to hang up when Michael spoke. "Susanna..."

"Yes."

"I'm glad you're back."

Elation swept through her. She'd thought about Michael non-stop the entire three days and nights she'd been gone, especially the long, drawn out nights. She was glad to know he'd missed her. "Me, too." When she hung up the phone, she couldn't help the happy grin that spread across her face.

"Hot date?"

Susan glanced up and laughed at the expectant look on her assistant's face. The younger woman stood in her doorway, twirling a strand of her short red hair between her fingers. That was why Callie made the perfect assistant. She was like a hound—always able to sniff out the good stuff.

"With Michael, it's guaranteed."

CR

A flute glass waited on the table in front of her as she sat down and draped her black fringed shawl over the back of her seat.

Susan arched an eyebrow and stared at Michael as the formal waiter set another flute glass on the table for Michael.

When the waiter pulled out a three-hundred-dollar bottle of champagne and poured her a glass, her eyes widened. "What are we celebrating?" she asked as he moved to fill Michael's glass.

Once they were alone, Michael raised his glass to her. "Here's to your new partnership. When you work that hard, you deserve to be acknowledged."

Susan swallowed the emotion that knotted in her throat. She hadn't even told Jason about her promotion because she didn't want to take away from the excitement of his pending wedding.

Lifting her glass, her smile trembled a little. "Thank you for making me feel special. I truly appreciate it."

"You're already special, Susanna. I'm just giving your accomplishment the due it deserves."

When the waiter returned with their menus, Susan asked, "So what's this secret project you're working on?" She took the proffered menu and returned her line of sight to Michael. His olive skin appeared even darker against his white shirt tonight. And the black suit he wore fit his broad shoulders as if it were made just for him. All she knew was...he looked damned good.

Michael's gaze traveled across her shoulders and down her exposed neck to the cleavage her black spaghetti-strapped dress revealed. Desire flickered in the deep brown depths when he met her gaze over his own menu. He waited for the waiter to walk away before he spoke.

"I never realized how alluring black looks against fair skin until this moment."

A shiver skidded along her back at his compliment. "And here I thought you asked me to wear black for that very reason."

"There is an added benefit, yes, but the truth is...we're going shopping."

Michael's wicked grin made her stomach flutter, but the shopping thing...now that surprised her. "Shopping? What kind of shopping are you planning to do?"

"I'm looking to make a deal."

"You don't strike me as a bargain hunter type."

Michael laughed and her pulse skittered at the genuine open boyishness his expression conveyed. "You could definitely say this is a long-standing bargain that needs to be addressed."

She shook her head at his enigmatic response. When he opened his menu, she did the same. No matter what Michael had in store for the rest of the evening, she had a feeling it wouldn't be dull.

CR

Susan glanced over her shoulder at the brown paper-wrapped package taking up most of Michael's back seat. Two hundred and fifty thousand dollars. Ohmigod. The man had just paid a small fortune for a painting. In an auction, no less. He'd bid on the landscape scene like a man on a mission, as if there was no way he was leaving that gallery without that painting in his hands. She had no doubt he would've paid more for it if he'd had to.

"That was interesting—" she started to say as Michael drove out of the museum parking lot.

"Do you remember me mentioning the investor who helped me start Piccoli's?"

Susan glanced down at Michael's firm hold on the gearshift as he moved it to the next gear. Lifting her gaze to stare at his profile in the dark car, she answered, "Yes. You said you've never bought him out because he was the one who believed and took a chance on you."

Michael cast a broad smile her way. "You paid attention."

She appreciated the respect reflected in his tone. Susan returned his smile and waited for him to continue.

"Charles Harrington invested in me when no one else would. I was so close to quitting, so close to losing faith that I had what it took to make my dream a success..." He paused for a second as if collecting himself, then let out a deep breath. "Charlie took a risk on me and never asked for anything in return."

When Michael's gaze returned to the road, Susan realized he was thinking deeply about his benefactor. She decided to let him tell her the rest when he was ready. That painting in the backseat had something to do with Charlie.

They'd traveled for fifteen minutes and entered an exclusive residential area before Michael pulled his sports car up to the curb along the tree-lined street and cut the engine. He got out of the car and walked around to her side. Opening the door, he offered his hand. "Ready to help me finally repay him?"

Susan followed Michael's gaze as he peered up the street. Wrought iron fencing edged several acres of land surrounding a beautiful brick mansion perched upon a hilltop.

Witnessing Michael's sense of duty and commitment to friendship firsthand dug a little deeper into her heart. She smiled as she put her hand in his and accepted his help out of the car. "I'd love to."

Her breath caught when his arm came around her back. He pulled her close and buried his nose against her neck. "I've missed your warmth and your smell these past few days, Susanna."

The cool night air didn't faze her with Michael's strong arms wrapped around her. She let a low laugh escape as she wrapped her arms around his shoulders. "Maybe it's a good thing I had to go out of town for work the day after you kept me up with our tantalizing phone conversation. I'd say the adage is true; absence does make the heart grow fonder."

"Your absence made me ache."

"Ditto," she whispered next to his ear before she pressed her lips against his cheek.

156

Susanna's Seduction

Michael kissed her neck then her jaw before his lips covered hers in a quick, hard kiss. "Duty first," he said as he stepped back.

Susan gave him a brilliant smile. She knew he had a hard time pulling away...just as much as she did. The sexual tension between them felt like a powerful magnetic pull.

She pushed the bucket seat she'd been sitting in forward and swept her arm toward the painting. "Am I right in assuming this painting has to do with Charlie?"

Michael grinned then leaned over and grabbed the painting. "Indeed it does."

She quietly followed him up the hill and waited while he punched in a code to get them through a back gate. Going in the back was kind of interesting. "Why didn't we just drive up to his front door?"

He chuckled as they continued up the sloped manicured lawn toward the huge home. "You don't know Charlie. As I said before, I would never buy him out, but do you have any idea how many times I've tried to give the man the money he invested in me all those years ago?"

She'd had to almost run to keep up with Michael's brisk pace, which wasn't an easy feat in heels, not to mention it was nighttime and she couldn't see where she stepped. "How many?" she panted out in a whisper. Dang, she hoped they didn't have dogs that left behind presents. She would have worn more sensible shoes if he'd told her they'd be traipsing through several acres of property tonight. There were lights on the four corners of the house, but they were still in the dark open field behind it.

"I've lost count over the years." He glanced at her and slowed his steps until she caught up with him. A few minutes later, they finally reached the cobblestoned patio. As Susan

157

stepped beside Michael onto the patio, bright lights flooded the surface.

When sudden brightness announced their stealthy arrival, she and Michael froze in unison. A second passed before he nodded and gave her a reassuring smile while glancing up at the floodlights. "Motion sensors."

She let out a sigh of relief and followed him forward, walking on her toes so her heels wouldn't clatter on the hard surface. Michael turned the knob on the French door and stiffened at the resistance.

"Damn. Sheila was supposed to have left this door unlocked."

Susan noted the disappointment in his tone. "Ah, so you elicited help from the inside, did you?"

"Charlie's wife knows how stubborn we both are. In answer to your question...yes, I did, but apparently someone came behind her and locked it."

"I didn't realize I'd be breaking and entering tonight. And here I thought you asking me to wear black had naughty, not nefarious connotations." She hoped her wry tone would lighten the situation and ease the tension that radiated from him.

"When it comes to you, every word out of my mouth could be a double entendre," he said with a wicked grin.

She smiled, glad to have brought his humor back. Staring at the lock, she opened her purse and dug around inside. "Is the alarm system turned off?"

He cast a curious gaze her way, nodding.

She pulled out her keys and unfolded a thin, flathead screwdriver from an all-in-one army knife that dangled from her keychain. When she dug out a couple of paperclips from the bottom of her purse and began to unbend them, she grinned at

Michael's perplexed expression.

"You should see the what-the-hell-is-she-doing look on your face." As she slung her purse over her shoulder, she explained, "I have an uncle with a big heart and a...colorful background. Before he went to prison—curse the man for his forever-sticky fingers—he taught my brother and me some skills I never thought I'd put to use. Well, except for that one time in high school when Marie Renee stole my softball glove. I knew she'd locked it away in her locker, so I took matters into my own hands."

"Naughty little Susan." Michael flashed her a devilish smile. He sounded almost pleased. Double entendre, indeed.

Susan gave a low laugh and started to work on the lock. "I'm sure Marie Renee thought I was a witch who had the power to spirit away her stolen goods." She winked at him then turned to focus on her task.

After a couple of minutes manipulating the pins inside the lock, she heard the lock's final pin click into place.

"You're just full of surprises," he murmured next to her ear as she turned the knob.

"Ever need your car hot-wired, I'm your woman. But...um...don't go advertising that. I have this whole 'Sensible Susan' reputation to uphold."

When she opened the door wide, she took in the rows of leather-bound books lining the floor-to-ceiling bookshelves, a couple of leather reading chairs and a large banker-style desk off to their left. Michael gave a low chuckle, drawing her attention.

"The fact your pristine halo is being held up by a cute set of horns will remain just between us." He tucked the huge frame under his arm and kissed her on the cheek before he walked past her into Charlie's study.

Susan's heart leapt at his brief, warm kiss. His quick wit made her smile. Intelligent, funny, sexy...the man hit all the right buttons. Putting away her improvised tools, she walked inside to stand next to him as he turned on a small lamp on the desk.

"Sheila said she and Charlie would leave at eight and not return for a couple of hours," Michael said in a low tone as he began to pull the tape away from the brown paper.

She set her purse down on the floor next to the desk and glanced at her watch. Eight-fifteen. They had plenty of time.

Working in companionable silence removing all the paper and tape, they'd just pulled the last bit of tape off the brown paper when a deep voice sounded down the hall—as if the person was approaching the office.

"Phillip won't give a rat's ass if we're late, Sheila."

Susan and Michael's gazes locked and widened in shock. As if an unspoken agreement swept between them, she gathered up all the tape and paper bits into a ball while Michael pulled the leather chair out from behind the desk and set the picture on the chair's arms.

"Charlie, this is ridiculous. See, yet another reason you should give up smoking." A woman's voice resounded from farther away as if she were yelling after her husband.

Michael grabbed Susan's hand and started to yank her toward a side door. She pulled her hand from his, scooped up her purse and followed him through the door he held open.

Charlie harrumphed. "You know my smoking is just recreational, but if I don't have at least one stogie to get me the hell outside and away from the stuffy riff-raff for a bit, we'll leave after half an hour. I swear it!"

Susan's breathing came in choppy gusts as she and Michael shouldered their way among the long, heavy coats
160

packed inside the closet until they found a small empty corner to squeeze into.

"Michael, the lamp," she whispered in a panic after she'd set her purse on the floor near her feet.

"Too late, love," came his low, amused response.

"What the hell..." Charlie's voice boomed throughout his office. "Sheeeeeeeila!"

"Yes, dear?"

"What's the meaning of this?"

Charlie didn't sound happy about the painting. Despite the wonderful sensation of Michael's body pressed against hers, the anger in the man's voice made Susan's entire frame tense. Her fingers curled around the brown paper ball.

Heels clicked on the hardwood floor then stopped as if a woman had stepped onto the carpet in the office. "It looks like a painting, honey."

"I'm going to kill the sonofabitch."

Michael chuckled close to Susan's ear then pressed his lips to the sensitive spot behind it.

Susan's stomach fluttered at the physical contact. If Michael wasn't bothered by the man's obvious rant, then she wouldn't let herself be, either.

Sheila laughed. "Darling, you're just angry Michael finally one-upped you. It's about time you accepted his appreciation."

Michael kissed her temple. Susan's libido kicked into full throttle when he continued kissing along her jaw toward her mouth.

"Damn it, but...she's a freakin' beaut, isn't she?" Charlie sounded so proud.

Michael's hands encircled Susan's waist. "She is indeed," he echoed Charlie's sentiment right before his mouth covered

161

hers. The thrust of his tongue against hers set her pulse thrumming.

"The painting is gorgeous and the perfect gesture. I'm sure Michael paid a pretty penny for it," Sheila replied.

Susan thrilled at the hot, all-consuming kiss. She so wanted to feel him inside her, thrusting deep. God, she craved his naked body pressing against hers, to feel his hard chest crushing her breasts, his hips spreading her thighs wide. Oral sex and mutual masturbation weren't going to cut it any longer. She let go of the ball of paper and thrust her fingers into Michael's hair to pull him closer and deepen their kiss.

"Probably way more than I initially invested in the sod," Charlie grumbled, his angry tone softening. "He knows I love him like a son. Why does he have to be so stubborn?"

"His stubbornness is the very reason you believed he could succeed, honey," his wife answered. "Do you think he has any idea how much you respect him?"

Michael pressed his hard body flush with Susan's, pushing her back flat against the wall as his tongue speared deeper, tasting all of her. The coats rustled with their movements, but Susan didn't care.

"Hell, no. I can't let him see my softer side."

Susan felt Michael's rakish smile against her lips. *I think he already knew that, Charlie*, she thought as she ran her tongue alongside Michael's.

"Come on, get your stogie and when we get back from the party, we'll find the perfect place to hang this painting. It's worth way more than the money Michael paid for it. After all...friendship is priceless."

The sound of a drawer opening filtered through the closed door at the same time Michael's hands gripped her waist tighter and he lifted her in the air. When he set her back against the

162

wall and ground his erection against her sex, she wrapped her legs around his waist.

Exquisite fluttering sensations rippled through her body at the friction and the feel of his hard cock grinding against her clit. Susan bit back the moan that threatened to escape. She was on fire. Her tongue parried with his as she rocked against him. Michael's heart pounded against hers at a rapid-fire rate.

The sound of more drawers opening and closing filtered through her foggy thoughts. She knew she was on the verge. Susan locked her heels at the base of Michael's spine and wrapped her arm tighter around his neck, pulling him closer. She couldn't get close enough. "I'm on the edge," she whispered, her voice breathy next to his ear.

Michael's heavy pants sent warm gusts of air down her throat. He continued his relentless, aggressive thrusting against her, his lips trailing across her jaw. His mouth hovered over hers as he paused his pistoning. "Come for me, Susanna."

"I—" She didn't even get out another word when he began to apply pressure, rubbing his cock in arousing circles against her. Susan's entire frame shook, wanting more. She clenched her sex, wishing he was deep inside her, but at this point, the pressure alone was enough to send her over.

He captured her lips with his, cutting off her scream as she climaxed. His fingers bit into her buttocks as rippling, goose bump-inducing, wave after wave of intense pleasure slammed through her, making her sex alternately ache and pulsate.

Susan swallowed her scream, but tears seeped from the corners of her closed eyes. As her orgasm slowed within her, she began to quake deep inside at the intensity of her attraction and total oblivion when she was with Michael. He made her forget everything; every inhibition she'd ever had slipped away the moment he touched her.

Never, not in a million years, would she have thought she'd have sex, make that semi-sex, while hiding in a closet with two people right outside the door. Michael made their near-public intimacy feel exciting, sexy and strangely natural.

"Hmm, I seem to have smoked my last one. Oh, wait, I think I have another box in the closet."

Susan and Michael froze at the comment that floated through the door as Charlie's voice came close and the doorknob began to turn.

Michael lowered her legs to the floor and whispered, "Busted." He rested his cheek against her forehead as they waited for the door to fling open.

"I think receiving this painting gives you plenty to talk about tonight. Skip the stogie. Let's go."

Charlie's deep chuckle sounded. "You're right. Can't wait to see the look on Phillip's face. He'd casually mentioned bidding for this particular painting himself, and if you hadn't had that flat tire, I'd have made the auction—" He cut himself off, his tone turning suspicious. "There wasn't an emergency, was there? No *good* Samaritan beat me to your rescue, did he? I'd assumed you'd somehow helped Michael get this painting in here tonight, but you were in this all along, weren't you?"

"I thought it was about time you accepted Michael's thanks. It means a lot to him that you do."

The man laughed outright. "Duped by my friend and my wife. Ha! I think I'll leave that part out of the story tonight. Come on. Let's go *wow* the crowd."

Michael let out a low "whew" as an outside door closed and silence greeted them. "You make a great partner in crime," he said against her cheek.

Her fingers flexed in his hair at his compliment. "You just like the perks having a sidekick allows."

"What can I say..." Michael's lips brushed against hers. "You're irresistible." He kissed her throat. "But as much as I find the idea of having full-fledged sex with you in a dark closet damned appealing...I want to make sure we won't be interrupted. How about we go back to my place and finish what we started?"

Michael's desire to take his time shook the taut hold she had on her emotions. She was glad he couldn't see the emotional tears she'd shed when she climaxed. Blinking back the tell-tale signs that he'd burrowed straight to her heart, she pulled him close and said, "I couldn't agree more," right before she kissed him.

As if he couldn't resist taking everything she offered, Michael slid his tongue aggressively against hers once more. He grasped her hips and began to rock against her in slow, purposeful thrusts for several seconds before he broke their kiss and said in a strained voice, "We'd better stop soon or our first time *will* be in a closet."

Susan's body shook from the desire Michael elicited within her. "To be honest, I'm past the point of caring where, but if you insist..." She started to withdraw her hands from his hair until she felt a tug.

"Ow!" Michael said.

When he tensed, something pulled at the skin on her palm and she realized what had happened. A piece of tape had stuck to her palm and was now imbedded in Michael's hair.

Susan tried to hold back her amusement at their situation, but failed miserably.

Chapter Six

When her laughter subsided, Michael opened the door then reached up and ripped the tape from his hair. He gritted his teeth at the pain. "That's one way to redirect my attention from the fact I'll be walking funny all the way back to the car."

Susan cast a sympathetic yet amused gaze his way. Gesturing toward the closet, she said, "We can always finish what we started in there..."

"Don't tempt me," he all but growled.

The look he gave her was so intense it swept her breath right out of her lungs in a quiet whoosh. Susan tingled all over at his husky, primal tone. She cast him a wicked grin and preceded him out the patio door, swinging her hips just a little more than she normally would.

She'd only taken a few steps before Michael grasped her hand. He pressed his warm lips against her knuckles briefly then started across the patio, pulling her with him. The fact he held her hand tight but didn't say a word turned her on even more. Her belly tensed and her core began to ache all over again in anticipation as she walked down the grassy slope beside him.

When they reached his car, Michael's fingers lingered at the base of her spine as he opened the car door for her. The tiny bit of contact was both intimate and incredibly arousing. She climbed inside the car and settled in the seat, wondering how far Michael's house was. The man had her so wrapped up she realized she'd never asked him where he lived.

Only the hum of the car's engine and the sound of Michael shifting gears filled the electric air between them as he drove to his home. It was as if neither of them wanted to talk—to break the magnetic attraction building between them.

The silence didn't stop Michael from casting his hooded gaze her way a few times. At the heated look she saw reflected in his eyes from an approaching car's lights, Susan gave him a sly smile.

They both knew what they wanted, and they'd damn well waited long enough to get there, she thought when he returned his gaze to the road. Why had he waited so long? The man had made his attraction to her very clear from day one.

In so many ways, from the very beginning, she knew Michael was a wonderful man. He'd sympathized with her over Melanie's "errand", had championed her in front of the whole rehearsal dinner crew and had basically been an all-around gentleman since she'd met him—like the fact he'd been the one to slow things down between them.

Susan furrowed her brow and cast her gaze out the window. Michael had said he wanted to get to know her. And in many ways he had, but did he know the real Susan? He'd seen a little of her tonight when she picked Charlie's lock, but as much as Susan abhorred being called "Sensible Susan", she knew she subconsciously worked hard to maintain that image...to keep an emotional distance.

The strong front she put on had given her a sense of authority over her kid brother throughout their years alone together. Her outward demeanor also demanded respect from her superiors and co-workers, not to mention it put a barrier around her heart six inches thick.

The reality was...as excited as she was by their upcoming evening, Michael scared her on many levels.

He was so confident and self-assured. She would have never propositioned him if the situation had been reversed. But he didn't hesitate...not once. He saw what he wanted and he became a part of her life...almost as if he'd always been a part of it. She wished she could be so carefree with her feelings.

What would he think when he finally met the real Susan? If they continued to spend time together, he would eventually see every facet of her personality, right down to the insecure and doubtful angles. She took a deep breath and relaxed her shoulders, forcing herself not to worry about the future and what-ifs. Tonight was about an enjoyable evening with a sexy man, not a lifetime commitment.

Right. If that was true, then why did Michael's spicy, seductive aftershave make her think how nice it would be to wake up to that scent every morning? She banished the indulgent thought from her mind, refusing to get attached to him.

She was so deep in her thoughts she lost track of time and place until Michael pressed a button on his steering wheel and the iron gates in front of them began to open. Susan sat up a little straighter as he drove through the gates and proceeded up the long drive. She smiled as she realized where he'd taken her. She should've known he lived in the Village.

When he parked his car in the circular driveway in front of his Manor-style home, Susan took in the huge white columns on either side of his front porch, the nice-sized balcony above the porch's roof and the plethora of windows on either side of the porch. Trees sprouted all around the cobblestone circular drive and a brick-lined fountain graced the center.

Once he cut the engine, the lone spotlight on the side of the house gave off very little light from the angle he'd parked, and darkness surrounded them. She unbuckled her seatbelt, and while electric silence stretched between them, the sound of the ocean's surf filtered through the closed windows, making Susan's skin prickle and her smile falter. Her dream came back to her full force.

I was about to go to a wedding, I love the beach...and Michael really wound me up that night before I went to bed. That's all it was, she told herself. "You have a beaut—"

Michael unbuckled his seatbelt and laid his hand on her neck, causing her to pause. She trembled as his thumb moved up the side of her throat to rub behind her ear. His heated touch soaked through her skin, igniting a fire within her. Susan let out a steadying breath before she finished, "—iful home."

"Welcome, Susanna," he said in a desire-filled voice before he pulled her close and covered her lips with his.

The sensuous slant of his lips devouring hers melted Susan's insides. She opened her lips and cupped her hands around his jaw, enjoying the sensation of his rough evening stubble against her palms.

Michael's tongue slid deep into her mouth, aggressive, but not forceful. He set a seductive, assertive pace that made her want to linger in the car and allow him to explore every crevice, every dip and hollow inside her mouth and beyond.

His hands darted in her hair and found the clip she'd secured it with. She felt it give way and heard a clatter as her clip hit the console before it fell to the floor.

"Impatient, are you?" She smiled against his lips as his fingers tunneled in her hair, unwinding the twist.

"I believe that'll be the understatement of the evening," he mumbled right before he gripped her shoulders and pulled her closer.

Susan let out a surprised yelp, but continued their kiss. Instead she nipped at his bottom lip and said in a husky voice, "Well, if you wanted me to come over, all you had to do was ask." She broke their kiss and climbed over the console. Michael tilted his steering wheel upward to give her room as she squeezed in front of it to settle on his lap.

The console dug into her left calf and she had to lower her head to keep from hitting the roof, but Susan didn't care. She chuckled as she moved her head beside his and whispered in his ear, "Hmm, this is a bit cozier than I expected."

Michael's right hand slid up her left thigh under her skirt at the same time the entire seat shifted back a good foot and a half.

"Comfortable?" he asked as he laid his other hand on her right thigh.

When his thumbs pressed on her inner thighs, flames swirled in her belly. The heated skin-against-skin contact of his fingers so very close to her aroused sex felt intimate and erotic. She pressed her mound against his erection, enjoying the feel of his hard cock rubbing against her damp silk panties and sensitized clit.

"Very cozy," she said right before she pressed her lips against his.

Michael's hands trailed up her back as he kissed her deeply. The distinctive sound of her zipper opening, along with the cool sensation of night air hitting her back, elicited a primal response in her. Susan moaned against his mouth and slid her hands into his thick hair, thrusting her tongue more aggressively against his.

Michael pulled her dress down her shoulders and then to her waist, exposing her bare breasts. She shuddered as the cool air puckered her sensitive nipples even more. When Michael's hands encircled her waist and he pulled her forward to press his face against her breasts, all she could do was clutch him close in surprise.

He turned his head and pressed his ear against her breastbone. "I've fantasized about the feel of your skin against mine, your heart's frantic beat underneath my cheek, and now that I have your provocative smell added to the mix...nothing compares."

His words and actions were so tender and reverent, they stole her breath. Susan's stomach fluttered. She closed her eyes and ran her hand through his hair, totally floored by the emotions this man's roughly uttered statement evoked in her.

Michael rocked his erection against her as his fingers pressed against her upper back. His heated breath warmed her breast right before his lips made contact.

Her heart ached as he kissed a slow, fiery path across the curve of her breast until his lips hovered over her nipple.

As she waited for his mouth to connect, Susan bit her lip in expectation. Need rose within her, clawing her belly, demanding that she move her body closer to him.

When he closed his mouth over her nipple and sucked on the hard peak with fervor, Susan clenched her fingers in his hair and let out a moan of sheer bliss. Pleasure radiated from her breast, jolting straight through her insides and ramming into her core.

She ground her sex against his cock and was stunned by the sense of rightness that slammed through her when he let out a deep groan against her breast.

Michael's hands moved to her ass and his fingers shoved past her underwear, grabbing the bare cheeks. His steel grip tightened and he jerked her harder against his upward thrusts.

"Damn, I hadn't planned to have sex in my car," he said as

his mouth moved to her other breast.

Michael had to release his hold on her nipple when she leaned back to unbuckle his belt buckle and unbutton his pants. Her breathing came in rapid pants while she pulled down his zipper. "If you think I'm waiting until we get inside, you can forget it."

Michael grabbed her wrist before her hand could connect with his erection. His dark gaze searched hers. "Are you sure, Susanna?"

She saw the raw hunger reflected in his gaze, even in the dim light. She didn't care that the seatbelt holder was digging into her knee or that the console was keeping her from fully wrapping her legs around this man the way she wanted to.

She gave him a half smile. "I want to feel you inside me, now, as deep as you can get."

Michael nodded and glanced toward the back seat where he'd tossed his jacket. "I have condoms in my jacket pocket. Can you reach them?"

"As long as you release my hand," she said with a laugh.

He rubbed his thumb over her pounding pulse then released her.

Susan tried to lean around the bucket seat, but her fingers couldn't quite reach the dark material. As it was, she was smashing her bare breasts against Michael's neck. Not that he seemed to mind.

Suddenly the seat began to tilt backward. Michael brushed his lips across her collarbone and chuckled. "Better?"

"Much." She grabbed hold of his jacket and felt around until she found the pocket. When her fingers touched several foil packets, she sat back up and faced him in triumph, condoms in hand.

"Mission accomplished."

He raised a dark eyebrow, his expression so hungry he made her tingle all over. "Not yet, sweetheart. Will you put it on for me?"

Her eyes widened. "You want me to put on your condom?"

He pulled his silk boxer briefs down, exposing his rigid erection. He grasped her free hand and wrapped her fingers around his thick cock.

When his other hand lifted her chin, Susan managed to unglue her gaze from the sight of her fingers gripping him tight. Her body shook with the need to have him inside her.

"I want to feel your hands around me as much as possible," Michael rasped.

His smoldering gaze yanked the air from her lungs. She'd never put a condom on a man before. Her past partners had always preferred to get the deed out of the way and then move on. None of them had ever suggested the act itself could be a pleasurable experience.

Susan's fingers closed around him and she began to slide them up and down his engorged cock.

Michael's fingers dug into her thighs. He closed his eyes for a brief second, laying his head back against the seat. His hips rocked in time with her movements and the groan that erupted from him made her feel incredibly powerful.

His head snapped up and his gaze lasered into hers. "You need to do it now, love."

Susan released her hold and peeled open the condom. Tossing the wrapper to the side, she placed the condom over the tip.

Instead of immediately sliding it over him, she ran her fingers, wet from the condom's lubrication, down his length, enjoying the feel of soft skin over steel hardness.

"Susanna," Michael gritted out, palming her ass once more.

Susan raised her eyes to his, loving the near-the-edge roughness in his voice. After she'd rolled the condom the rest of the way down, she put her hands on his shoulders and pressed her breasts against his chest, whispering in his ear, "How much do you want it?"

"More than you'll ever know," he replied at the same time he gripped her underwear, yanked it to the side then guided her hips lower.

She shivered deep inside at this primal side she was seeing of Michael. She liked it!

As she lowered herself over him and his impressive cock began to stretch her in wonderful, delicious ways, Michael kissed her neck and rocked his hips upward, thrusting deeper inside her.

Her body broke out into a fine sheen of sweat and her inner walls clenched as she gripped his shoulders tight. Shoving her hips downward, she buried his cock deep inside her. Jaw-grinding deep.

The act sent her right over the edge. As her orgasm splintered around her and her heart thumped in erratic beats, she tensed and held her body as still as she could. She didn't want to send Michael too soon into his.

"It's not working, love. You're clamping onto me like a fucking glove—God, you...feel...good!"

Michael's breathing turned choppy as he began to rock his hips forcefully, jerking upward and deeper inside her. Susan finally moved, meeting each of his thrusts with downward counter movements. She'd never felt so full before, not to mention the fact his actions were rubbing his pelvic bone against her clit, the erotic sensations sending her to a new plane of bliss.

Her body heat spiked and she panted as she dug her nails into his shoulders, slamming down on him hard. When Michael nipped at her collarbone and then her neck, she keened her excitement and squeezed her muscles around him.

Michael shuddered then let out a primitive growl as he came. His thrusts went impossibly, claim-stakingly deep as his fingers bit into her rear, his strength pulling her even tighter against him. Susan's orgasm ricocheted through her in a never-ending tidal wave of pulsing sensations. By the time the contractions ended, her thighs trembled and her entire body shook. She closed her eyes, almost overwhelmed at the sheer heat, intensity and depth of their lovemaking—as if they were subconsciously trying to fuse their bodies together.

When Michael ran his tongue up the middle of her chest, swiping away sweat that had formed between her breasts, Susan gasped and held the back of his head, loving his attentive nature. Her eyes slowly opened and the sight of the windows' condition shocked her. The glass was completely fogged to the point condensation rolled down the slick surface.

Michael kissed her neck then her jaw, saying in a husky tone, "Even your sweat tastes like an aphrodisiac. It's just the right amount of musky sweetness."

Susan met his steady gaze and spoke, her voice shaky. "I knew we'd be good together, but I had no idea we'd—"

"Connect?" he answered for her, his expression serious. "I had no doubts, Susanna." He gave a wry smile as he cast his gaze around the car. "Though I didn't expect our first time to be in a car like a couple of hormonal teenagers."

"I never could've predicted that one," she said with a wink as she carefully moved off him, over the console and back in her seat.

Tossing Michael a tissue pack from her purse, she grabbed her hair clip off the floor and dropped it into her purse. As he straightened his pants, she adjusted her underwear and pulled her dress back up on her shoulders.

Once she was presentable, she turned her back to him and glanced over her shoulder, "Will you zip me up?"

Once he'd zipped up her dress, Michael leaned close and whispered in her ear, "I don't know why I'm bothering. I'm just going to unzip it again the first chance I get."

Chill bumps formed on her skin at his promise. "Then you'll have something to look forward to," she teased before she put her purse on her shoulder and opened the car door.

Michael's deep chuckle followed her out of the car, keeping her warm against the breezy, cool night air. She couldn't help but smile. The man made her feel so good. He made her feel...special.

"Care to let me in on the secret?" he asked as he came around the car and handed her the wrap she'd left behind.

Susan took her wrap and stared into his eyes. "No secrets, just happy to finally spend some time alone with you."

Michael kissed her forehead then clasped her elbow in a warm grip. "Me, too."

Susan allowed him to escort her up the walkway, smiling as the path lit with each step they took toward the front door. "Motion detectors," she said. "Nice touch." Excitement grew within her once they reached the front door. She was curious to know the type of home Michael would pick for himself.

He unlocked the door and as she entered the foyer, she gasped at the beautiful, open design. It might look like a traditional manor home on the outside, but she loved the huge atrium-style room that greeted them. With the exception of a wide staircase that came down the center of the room, she could see straight through to the backside of the house from one side of his home to the other. Huge picture windows went all the way up to the ceiling and only a catwalk on the second level blocked her view. From what she could see, it appeared the catwalk hallway connected one side of the house to the other on the second floor.

Michael flipped a switch on a side wall and the oversized chandelier above them came on. He touched another switch and the lights dimmed to candlelight strength. Taking her wrap and purse, he set them on a dark walnut hall table. His fingers laced with hers and he pulled her farther into the living room on the right side of the house. Her heels clicked on the polished wood floor until she stepped onto the area rug in the living room.

The bit of light from the entryway allowed her to see the room boasted warm browns, reds and touches of honey-colored pillows on plush, buttery–soft, light brown leather furniture. A stone fireplace took up the right wall along with built-in shelves that boasted cabinet space underneath. Michael picked up a remote control from the oval glass-topped coffee table and pressed a button.

Saxophone accompanied a piano as jazz music floated from all corners of the room. He hit another button and floodlights came on outside, giving her a gorgeous view of a split-level deck that spanned the entire back of the house.

"Do you want me to turn on the lights?" Michael asked, looking down at her.

She shook her head. "No, I like listening to the surf in the dark."

His white teeth flashed in the dim light and he lowered the music before he set down the remote. "I'll be right back."

She smiled, chill bumps of excitement forming on her arms

as she watched him walk toward a closed door. When he stepped through the swinging door, she caught a glimpse of a sterling-front refrigerator. *What* does *the man have in store for me?*

Once Michael was out of sight, Susan's gaze landed on the other half of the darkened house. With ceiling-to-floor built-in bookshelves flanking either side of a movie-sized projector screen and a built-in stereo system that had to cost at least fifteen grand, she decided the other room was a combo library/entertainment room.

The surf pounding the beach outside drew her attention, making her wish it wasn't fall. If she could hear the waves, she knew his house had to pretty much be right on the beach, even if she couldn't see the sand or the white foam the waves usually left behind. If it were summer, she'd insist they walk the beach tonight, hand-in-hand. She'd relish the feel of the sand squeezing between her toes and a sexy man by her side. Nothing more committed than that!

Susan slipped out of her shoes and closed her eyes for a few seconds as she dug her toes in the carpet and imagined the sand between her toes.

When Michael wrapped his arms around her waist and pulled her back against his chest, her heart sped up. She let out a soft sigh and settled against his hard warmth, folding her arms over his. "I'm incredibly jealous. You get to see the beach every day. The view must be breathtaking."

He nuzzled her neck and his arms lightly squeezed her waist. "I have a spectacular view of the sunrise. I hope you'll watch it with me in the morning."

She glanced at him, her eyebrow raised in question.

A serious expression settled on his face as he turned her around in his arms. His fingers laced against her spine and he pulled her flush with his hips. "Yes, I want you to stay."

Chapter Seven

The man left her absolutely speechless. What was it about him that swept away her ability to form a coherent sentence, let alone a witty comeback? At the moment, no one would guess she could be a hell of a negotiator in the board room, spinning a tale about her client that would have potential supporters salivating to close the deal before anyone else could scoop them.

Then she realized what it was about Michael that drew her in. Sure he was sexy as hell, but the man wore confidence like a very comfortable second skin. Not only was he self-assured in his professional life, but when it came to his personal one, he went after what he wanted, no-holds-barred.

"Are you always so confident?" she found herself asking with a half smile as she stared into his penetrating gaze.

Michael leaned close and inhaled near her neck. "When it comes to you...yes. I knew the moment I looked into your gorgeous blue eyes we'd be very good together."

Her breath caught at his sexy comment, and her body tingled all over when his hands shifted to the bare skin on her shoulders to press her upper body closer to his. It was as if he couldn't get close enough to her. Susan wrapped her arms around his neck then slid her fingers into his hair. Pressing her nose against his throat, she inhaled the seductive scent that was all Michael.

"Say you'll stay," he said in a low tone.

"Promise I'll see the sunrise?"

"Guaranteed." He stepped back and laced his fingers with hers before tugging her along behind him.

"Where are we going?" She allowed him to lead her toward the French door in the corner of the room.

He opened the door, and the sound of the waves slamming against the shore made her body sing. "Taking you where you can hear the surf," he replied, pulling her outside onto a deck that spanned the entire backside of his home.

Susan laughed and tugged against his hold. "But it's fifty degrees out here. We'll freeze our asses off."

She caught his amused grin as he turned her away from him. Placing his warm hands on her shoulders, he gave them a gentle squeeze. "Then you'd better get rid of these clothes."

The cool wind caused chill bumps to form on her arms. Susan held her hands over her bare arms while Michael slid the first spaghetti strap down her shoulder.

His comment made absolutely no sense. "You're cra...zy," she said through chattering teeth while suppressing the giggle that threatened to surface.

"Only about you." His lips connected with her shoulder as he pulled the other strap down, then unzipped the back of her dress. "Move your hands, Susanna. I want to see all of you."

Sudden warmth swept through her from his statement and the need that resonated in his voice. She allowed her hands to fall and her dress slid down her curves to land in a rumpled pile at her feet.

Michael grasped her hand and spun her around to face him. The hungry look in his gaze sweeping swept over her entire body stole her breath.

Patrice Michelle

"You're gorgeous," he murmured.

The cool, salty air licked her nipples, making them pucker instantly. She did her best not to shiver under his intense stare. Instead she slipped out of her underwear and stepped close to him. Wrapping her arms around his waist, she tilted her head so she could stare into his eyes. "You're a bit overdressed."

He slid his hands down her spine, palming her bare butt. When his fingers flexed on her skin and he pulled her flush against his erection, Susan gasped and her body tingled.

"Let's take care of you first," he said before he quickly lifted her in his arms and carried her toward a stone wall on the side of the deck. A rumbling sound, different from the surf in the background, caught her attention.

Susan gripped Michael tight around the neck as he descended a few wooden stairs then turned to walk past where the stone wall had ended.

When her gaze landed on the bubbling hot tub, she shot a wide grin his way. Taking in the unique oasis of flowers and plants that surrounded the oversized tub that looked more like a small pool, she said, "It's perfect," the moment he lowered her feet into the heated water.

As she stepped to the deeper side of the tub and lowered herself into the welcoming warmth, he shook his head. "Not quite."

Kicking off his shoes, he walked over to a panel on the side of the house and hit a couple of buttons. The light behind him doused right before the turbulent bubbles on the surface ceased, leaving only a few of the lower jets circulating the water.

On the other side of the wall the deck's light gave off a dim glow in the hot tub's area. For a couple of suspended seconds, complete silence greeted her ears. Then the ocean waves filtered into her consciousness. Her heart swelled and Susan closed her

182

eyes so she could listen to the soothing sound.

"I'm in heaven." She tilted her head back and waved her arms in the water.

"My thoughts exactly."

Michael sounded closer. She opened her eyes to see him squatting on the side of the tub, holding a wine glass out to her.

Her body ignited when her wet fingers brushed against his to retrieve the glass. She knew without looking that it was merlot.

Michael reached out and tucked a strand of her hair behind her ear. His fingers caressed her jaw before he rested his forearm on his knee. "It's a reserve I've kept for a special occasion."

His words warmed her. She didn't want to think about how many other women Michael might have had in this very same hot tub. For tonight she wanted to believe she was the only one who mattered.

Susan took a sip of her wine while Michael stood. He'd left his jacket in the car, and the sight of him unbuttoning his shirt made her pulse skitter.

Smiling in the darkness, she called his name in a quiet voice, then set her glass on the deck and pressed her breasts against the side of the tub to look up at him.

"Hmm?" he asked.

She beckoned him closer with a crook of her finger and a sexy, come-hither look.

When he put his knee on the deck and leaned close, Susan ran her hands along his shirt over his chest. "You have waaaay too many clothes on," she said right before she tugged on the cotton material, pulling him into the water beside her.

Water sloshed and overflowed onto the deck from Michael's

abrupt entry. Susan laughed at the sopping wet sight he made erupting from the water, his dark hair down in his eyes.

When Michael pushed his hands across his face, shoving his wet hair back, his intense expression cut off her laughter. Her lungs seized as he ripped his shirt off and threw it on the deck with a wet plop. He advanced on her, and she stepped backward against the edge of the hot tub.

Her gaze locked with his as Michael placed his hands on the deck on either side of her, caging her in. Placing her elbows on the tub's edge, she leaned back a little when he leaned forward. "Surely you're not mad?" She kept her tone light-hearted.

He held her wine glass in front of her. "Wine goes well with dessert, and I see a perfect place to start," he said, tilting the glass.

The red liquid hit her right in the hollow of her throat before sliding down between her breasts.

Susan tingled all over when he grasped her waist. Her hands moved to grip his muscular arms and she let her head fall back as he leaned down to suck the wine from the small indention.

His lips connected with her skin, and she shuddered while sheer desire shot to every part of her body. Despite the cool air around her, she was on fire. Michael nipped at her neck and her body molded to his as if she were literally melting into him.

"You'll just have to figure out how to remove the rest of my clothes," he said in a low, sexy tone as he gripped her upper back and lifted her slightly in the water.

When he lapped at the wine streaks between her breasts, her fingers moved of their own accord to his wet hair. She cupped his head at the same time she wrapped her bare legs around his hips. His mouth connected with one of her nipples and pleasure splintered though her, making her gasp. Pressing her mound against his erection, she gyrated her hips against him. "I have a feeling you can get your pants off faster than I can."

"Ah, but the point is...I want *you* to take them off." Releasing her breast he walked backward while holding her close. He stopped walking when the height of the water stopped at his mid-thigh. Lifting her completely away from him, he slowly set her down in the water.

The intensity in his gaze hadn't changed, but this time she recognized it for what it was...pent-up arousal. Susan had never felt more sexually powerful than she did at that moment.

She slowly slid her hands across his chest, pausing to appreciate every dip and contour his muscles created before she moved her fingers down his hard abs. When his stomach muscles flexed, her gaze jerked to his, but Michael's eyes were closed, his jaw tense. Susan watched his face as she moved her fingers to unbutton his pants. The soaked fabric made sliding the zipper open difficult, but not impossible.

As soon as she tugged the wet material down Michael's hips, revealing his underwear molded to his erection, his gaze seared into hers and his hands cupped her face. Running his thumbs along her jawline, Michael pulled her close and covered her lips with his. Susan craved his taste, his touch, his closeness. Her mouth opened under his, welcoming the aggressive thrust of his tongue.

She could hear the ocean's waves above the quieter rush of hot tub bubbles surfacing from below, and when Michael's lips met hers, all her senses sharpened. She tasted the salt in the air, smelled the secrets of the ocean surrounding her, making her feel a part of the incessant waves crashing against the shore, moving in perfect time with her wild heartbeat.

Michael's hands speared into her hair and he cradled the back of her head as he slanted his mouth over hers, deepening their kiss. The coolness of his skin combined with his internal heat pressed against her front and the brisk wind blowing against her back made her shiver and tremble all at once. He kissed her like he couldn't get enough of her taste, as if he wanted to make sure he left behind an indelible part of himself when their lips finally separated.

The hot water surrounding her sex made it sensitive and swollen. Her channel throbbed with heat from his possessive kiss and the tense dominance in the way he held her...like he never planned to let her go. This kiss was different from any other time he'd kissed her. It was more intimate and thorough, almost soul-searching in its intensity, eliciting an emotional response she hadn't expected...desire for permanence. She knew she was caught up in the moment, but she reveled in the fantasy as she ran her fingers over his erection through his underwear to stoke his arousal even more.

Michael gripped the back of her neck and placed his forehead on hers as his other hand moved to palm her hip in the water. His heavy breathing made her smile. She kissed his jaw, then she slid her hand down his hard cock to grasp his sac. His hips rocked, encouraging her.

She trailed her nails down his back and dug them into his butt to pull him closer, while she wrapped her fingers around the bulge, grasping his erection. She felt his groan rumble in his chest as she kissed his pectorals then moved her lips down the center of his cut abs. Feathering kisses lower, she tugged his underwear down and then pushed his wet clothes even further down his thighs.

As soon as his cock sprang free of his clothes, Susan ran her tongue around the tip. He tasted of salt and chlorine, and musky male. She paused in her efforts to remove his clothes, wrapping her warm mouth around the tip of his erection.

Michael's hand gripped the back of her head and he moaned when she took him deep inside her mouth. His fingers wound in her hair as she used her tongue to caress him. Rocking forward, he sent his cock deep into the recesses of her mouth, his body tensing. She loved the feeling of power his response gave her.

She ran her tongue all the way down his length and closed her lips tight before she began to apply arousing suction all the way up his hard length. His breathing turned shallow right before he gripped her shoulders and pulled away from her mouth, surprising her. Susan gave him a confused look. Surely he wanted her to continue.

"You're right, I can do it faster."

The intense, on-the-edge look in his expression made her shudder. While he finished removing his pants, she turned away to retrieve the glass of wine from the side of the tub.

"The bottle is by the stairs," Michael answered her unspoken question when she picked up the almost empty glass.

Placing her knees into the contoured seat off to the right of the stairs, she retrieved the bottle and filled her glass. She'd just set the bottle back down when Michael's pants made a loud plop on the deck next to the bottle.

The sight of the condom wrapper landing beside his pants caused her heart rate to kick up several more notches. Not to mention the fact her rear end was currently on display in the cool night air. She set her glass on the side of the tub and started to lower herself all the way back into the water when Michael's firm hands grasped her hips.

"Stay put."

Her body throbbed as he massaged her bare buttocks. She gripped the side of the tub in front of her and closed her eyes in sheer delight when his fingers slid between her legs.

"I've never seen a more inviting picture."

His dark tone made her shiver while he trailed a feathery touch closer to her core. Susan arched her back and clenched her lower muscles, waiting...dying for him to touch her.

When he slid a finger straight past her opening to ride her clit, her hips moved, encouraging him. A soft whimper bubbled past her closed lips, despite her effort to keep quiet.

"Don't hold back, Susanna. I want to hear your cries, to know you want me as much as I want you," he said at the same time his hands gripped her hips. He guided her hips lower until his erection pressed against her opening.

Skin prickling, her pulse thrumming, she dug her fingernails into the wood flooring around the tub and clenched her muscles around the tip of his cock in excited anticipation.

"You feel perfect," he groaned at the same time he pulled her off the seat and toward him, driving his cock deep inside her.

"Oh, God," she panted out as her feet touched the tub floor. Michael's deep penetration had set her on the verge of a climax. Her arms shook and her heart beat at an out of control pace. The sheer ecstasy that rippled through her at their joining was almost overwhelming.

With one hand clasping her hip, Michael moved his other to her bare breast and leaned over her back, surrounding her with his heat. "Not yet, my sweet Susanna. Wait a little longer," he said close to her ear, then kissed her temple with a gentle brush of his lips.

Every nerve ending in her body flexed and jumped, ready to pounce and push her headlong into orgasm. She was on fire, her fingers and toes full of needles as he rolled her nipple between his fingers, once, twice. He gave the hard bud a pinch, and her breath hitched. She whispered his name at the erotic connection radiating from her breast to her core. When she clenched her inner muscles hard and heard his hissing intake of breath, she managed a smile. "Are you sure you want to wait?" she teased, then began to slowly move her hips back and forth.

Grasping her hips to stop her movements, Michael pressed her body forward until her pelvis touched the front of the seat. "You'll thank me later." His low baritone rumbled in her ear as he slid her feet farther apart with his foot then laced his fingers with one of her hands on the side of the tub.

"This feels wonderful," she managed to pant out as he laid his chest across her entire back to push a button on the side of the tub.

All the tub's jets came on again as he threaded his other hand with her free one. She felt the jet pounding on her stomach, but didn't have time to miss the sound of the surf drowned out by the bubbles as Michael began to move in and out of her.

With each thrust her body zinged, spiraling tighter and tighter. His lips grazed her neck and the sound of his labored breathing turned her on even more.

The cool air caused a new round of goose bumps to form on her skin and her nipples to harden to pulsing nubs. The myriad of sensations was so intoxicating. She ached all over for release.

Then Michael's grip tightened on her hands and he flexed his arm muscles, tugging her hands farther away from them, lifting her higher.

Pounding water suddenly invaded her sensitive clit when the jet hit her dead on. Susan's panting turned to choppy gusts at the oh-so-sweet onslaught.

"Oh, God, Michael...I can't...oh, God..."

Her toes were barely touching the bottom of the hot tub, giving her very little choice but to take whatever Michael chose to dish out. And it felt so ever-lovin' good!

His hips ground against her buttocks and his thrusts grew harder, more demanding. Perfect friction and stimulation surrounded her, front to back, igniting all her senses. And then his words undid her...

"Come for me, Susanna. I want to hear you scream out, to feel you gripping me like you never want to let me go."

"I don't," she answered honestly right before a scream erupted from her lips unlike any she'd ever heard before. Susan climaxed in body-encompassing shudders over and over to the point she wondered if she would survive Michael's intense lovemaking.

She was so out of it, her body so sensitized, she was glad his tense arm muscles had relaxed enough to allow her feet to touch the bottom once more. No longer inundated with dual sensations, she was able to concentrate on moving against him while he pistoned twice more inside her, his fingers gripping her hands tight. A guttural groan rushed past his lips as he pressed her hard against the tub with his own climax, then collapsed against her back, his breathing just as heavy as hers.

Susan lifted one of his hands to her lips and kissed his knuckles. "I can honestly say I've never felt anything like that before."

Michael gave a low chuckle and untangled his hands from hers. Clasping her breasts, he guided her to a standing position and pulled her back against his chest. He ran his lips up her neck then planted an achingly possessive kiss on her jaw. "I have all night to discover the many ways to make you scream, and I intend to explore every one of them."

His sexy promise made her shiver, but she wasn't about to

let him think this would be a one-sided deal. Sliding her hand between them, she clasped his sac and ran her fingers down the middle at the same time she cupped his bare buttock with her other hand. "Turnabout is definitely fair play. I always give as good as I get."

Michael turned her in his arms and locked his hands at the base of her spine. The man's devilish grin made the butterflies in her belly lift and swirl like helpless leaves in a strong wind.

"I'm looking forward to it," he said right before his lips met hers.

Chapter Eight

Michael woke to the sensation of Susan's warm body curled up beside him in his bed. Glancing at his clock, he saw he had forty minutes before the sun began to rise. He turned his bedside lamp on low and leaned on his elbow to watch her sleep for several minutes. Her blonde hair was a tangled mess spread out on his pillow. He picked up a few strands and pulled them toward his nose, inhaling her appealing scent. She smelled like home: rumpled fresh-laundered sheets, faint remnants of his bath soap and her own sexy, feminine smell.

He ached as his gaze traveled her slender nose, to her high cheekbones and full mouth. As much as the ache had to do with his arousal whenever she was near, the sensation moved deeper into his gut. He realized why he'd been so determined to delay having sex with Susan. It had very little to do with his last relationships and everything to do with the fact this woman got under his skin.

She went to bat for the ones she loved, no matter her own reservations. She was fun, smart, sexy...everything he wanted in a woman. He'd always thought his career would be his first and last love...until the day she walked into his restaurant and blew him away.

He pulled back the sheet, exposing her naked upper body. Running his fingers along her soft skin, he relished the difference in their skin tones—his dark and hers fair.

Last night proved everything his body had been telling him. Not only were they matched intellectually, but their sexual chemistry was as explosive and fundamentally satisfying as it could get.

She moaned in her sleep and rolled over onto her back. The erotic sight of her naked body sprawled in his bed, her warm, pink nipples hardening as they reacted to the cooler air, made him throb. He wanted her to start this new day the way yesterday ended...in sheer pleasure.

☙

Susan dreamed of Michael's hands on her body...his heavy weight pressing her to the bed as his cock thrust deep, spreading her walls wide. She rocked her hips in blissful pleasure at the sensations swirling through her.

The dream changed and Michael's warm breath bathed her skin as he kissed a seductive path up her inner thigh toward her sex.

With a blissful sigh, she let her legs fall to the bed in total surrender...

The jostling of the bed jerked her eyes open at the same time Michael's lips connected with her entrance.

Susan gasped, loving the exquisite building sensations rippling through her with each swipe of his tongue against her clit. She arched her back and pressed her body closer, moaning as he began to suck on the firm nub.

Michael lifted his head and cast his gaze toward the sliding glass doors near the bed. "The sun will rise soon. I thought you might want to be awake to see it."

He looked so sinfully sexy with his black hair all askew. She sat up on her elbows and followed his line of sight before returning her gaze to his. "I couldn't have asked for a better alarm clock." She laughed when he gripped her rear end and yanked, pulling her back down onto the bed, but her amusement changed to a whimper as he slid a finger deep inside her body and pressed on her g-spot.

She dug her heels into the mattress and lifted her hips in time to the rhythmic slide of his finger moving inside her. Last night with Michael had been like something out of an erotic fairy tale. The man made passionate love to her all night long. His attentive nature made her feel incredibly sexy and special.

In return, she'd given herself over completely to their lovemaking, giving him as much pleasure as he did her. She lay in Michael's bed last night with her head on his chest and her legs entwined with his. Snuggling close to his masculine warmth felt so natural, she instantly fell into an exhausted sleep. She'd never done that with another man. In the past, after having sex, her mind whirled for hours before she could finally close her eyes.

As Michael ran his tongue along swollen, sensitive folds and across her clit, he added another finger to the one penetrating her. Her breath caught. She bucked and moaned from the whirlwind of erotic sensations swirling inside her body. Tightening her stomach muscles, she clenched her channel around his fingers, her actions adding to the friction he provided. At the same time his lips latched onto her clit, Michael slid another finger down her slit and pressed against that soft spot just below her entrance.

Every part of her sex was on fire with sensations. Susan screamed out, reveling in the unique combination of his mouth and his knowing touch sending pleasurable pinpricks scattering from her core and upward throughout her body.

Her climactic contractions were both rapid and intense, sending her breath rushing through her lungs in frantic pants of keening rapture.

When her tremors stopped, she ran her fingers through his hair as he withdrew his hand from her body and pressed a light kiss against the bit of blonde hair on her mound. She expected him to move over her and rub his erection against her, enticing her to want to please him, but he didn't.

"I always keep my promises," Grabbing her hand, he pulled her off the bed and tugged her toward the sliding glass doors. Once he pushed the sheer curtains back, he moved behind her and wrapped his arms around her waist. Susan settled her back against his warm, hard chest and waited for the sun to rise.

"Your sunrise, coming right up," he whispered next to her temple.

As the sun began to rise over the water, its deep orange and pink colors reflecting in elongated ovals across the rippling surface, she smiled, feeling more contented and comfortable with this man than she'd ever been before with her past lovers.

She dug her fingers into his muscular thighs and ran her nails up the sides before she slipped her hands behind her and grasped his erection. Curling her fingers around his hard length, she slid her hand all the way to the base and back up at a slow pace. "I think we can make it a perfect sunrise, don't you?"

❧

After a long, drawn out shower with Michael, Susan wrapped his thick white robe around her and brushed her teeth with the new toothbrush he'd left on the counter for her before he went downstairs, saying, "It pays to have a dentist in the family." As she padded down the stairs, she chuckled in memory of the huge box of toothbrushes she'd seen under the sink's cabinet when she threw away some tissue.

Michael met her at the bottom of the stairs wearing navy lounge pants and a sexy grin as he held out a steaming black coffee mug for her. Standing on the bottom stair, she was eye to eye with him. The unique vantage point allowed her to view the morning sun reflecting on his pitch black hair. Intriguing blue streaks highlighted the wet strands, reminding her of raven's feathers.

Smiling at her fanciful thoughts, she wrapped her fingers around the warm mug while her gaze slid over his angular, clean-shaven face. "Thank you. It smells delicious. Do you have any cream?"

He stepped close and lifted some of her hair, inhaling. "You smell good enough to eat." His predatory gaze swept over her while he slowly rubbed the damp blonde pieces between his fingers. The possessive appreciation in his gaze conveyed how much he enjoyed seeing her in his robe. "I'll be right back with the cream."

Susan shivered at the loss she experienced the moment he stepped away and headed for the kitchen. Shaking off the odd sensation, her line of sight drifted to the open living room and caught on the sun reflecting off the glass-fronted built-in cabinets lining the far wall. She took a sip of her black coffee, wrinkled her nose at the strong taste—needed cream—and entered the living room. As she headed toward the cabinet, she instantly recognized several of the bright colors behind the glass doors.

Board games.

Stacked neatly on the cabinet shelves behind the glass, she

saw Parcheesi, chess, checkers, backgammon, Life, Monopoly, Trivial Pursuit and the list went on and on. Michael had every classic game she'd ever remembered playing growing up.

"I've been collecting them for fifteen years." Michael set the container of cream on the desk in front of them and wrapped his arm around her waist, pulling her back against his chest. His low voice sent a thrill zinging through her. "Do you collect anything? Or have a hobby?"

She'd honestly thought he was joking when he'd said he collected board games. Her grip tightened on the coffee mug. She wasn't used to telling others much about herself at this level, yet Michael made her feel like he genuinely wanted to know.

Nodding, she answered his question. "I collect fairies. My parents started giving me figurines as a child and well, after I lost mom and dad in the car accident, keeping the collection going was my way to remember them—like my parents lived on, watching over me through the little sprites' magical eyes."

She laughed softly. "I know it sounds silly, but it helped me cope with being an 'instant' mom at such a young age. You should see the collection of figurines I have in a curio cabinet at home. I'm going to have to buy another case soon."

"Fairies... You look like one yourself." His arms tightened around her and he kissed the back of her head.

Her cheeks warmed at his compliment. Glancing up at him, she asked, "What about you? Why do you collect board games?"

"To me board games symbolize togetherness with friends and family." Gesturing toward the cabinet, he elaborated. "I like what these bright packages represent—lots of laughter, good-natured competition and general good times."

Susan loved his philosophy. Seeing all those board games brought back many fond memories from her childhood. She leaned against his warmth, glad he wasn't able to see her misty eyes. "My parents, Jason and I would play Life and Monopoly for hours. When we got older, Jason and I used to have backgammon tournaments."

Releasing her, Michael opened the cabinet and picked up the backgammon game. When he broke the cellophane wrapper and began to pull it off the leather bound case, she gasped. "What are you doing? That's a first addition."

Michael gave her a devastating smile. "As I said, board games are meant to bring friends and family together. Grab the cream and I'll meet you at the table in the kitchen. We'll have our own tournament."

As he walked away carrying the game, he called over his shoulder, "Get ready to be stomped. Winner gets to pick how *he* wants to be spoiled for the day."

Her competitive nature shoved all the sentimental memories to the back of her mind. Grabbing the creamer, she quickly followed after him. "You don't have a prayer, Piccoli."

CR

Michael smiled at her as she smoothed her skirt for the twentieth time. "You look great," he said with a wink.

They'd been going out for a month and a half now, and every time she was with Michael, he'd planned a new adventure, from hiking to football games to yep, lots of roller coaster rides. And the sex, God, the sex was out of this world, curl-your-toes exceptional! Their chemistry was so tangible, so electric she worried she'd become addicted to the man.

She'd been surprised and pleased when Michael invited her to have dinner with his family. But now that she was standing on the Piccolis' front porch waiting for Michael's parents to answer the door, she found her throat closing with nerves.

As she started to rub away another imaginary wrinkle in her skirt, Michael grabbed her hand and kissed her knuckles. "Just be yourself, Susanna."

The door opened and a tall man with thick salt and pepper hair smiled at her. "You must be Susanna. I'm David, Michael's father. Come on into the kitchen. We've got the wine, cheese and crackers ready to go."

Susan gave Michael a tremulous smile as he put his hand on her back and ushered her inside.

The smell of rich marinara sauce and garlic bread welcomed her, inviting her into the huge kitchen that was full of people.

Taken aback, Susan glanced at Michael, her eyes wide and her chest quickly seizing at the sheer number of people. She counted at least ten, and she'd only expected to have dinner with his parents.

Wrapping his arm around her waist, Michael grinned. "Meet my family, Susanna...all ten and a half of them," he said as a very pregnant woman with long black hair approached and handed Susan a glass of wine.

"Hi, Susan. I'm Rachel, Michael's sister-in-law." She pointed to a stocky, dark-haired man with a goatee who was leaning against the center island and stuffing a breadstick in his mouth. "That's my husband, Keith." She moved closer and whispered, patting her round belly, "He seems to believe this 'eating for two' philosophy extends to him as well." Pointing to a thin man and a blonde woman, she said, "That's Joshua and Kelly and the short, spiky-haired guy with glasses is Jonathan. His wife, Sherri, is the cute redhead with a temper to match her coloring. Sean's easy to pick out. He's the only one with light brown hair. We tell him he's secretly adopted and light hair on an Italian is why he's still single."

"I heard that, Rachel," Sean called from a few feet away. Stealing the steaming breadstick Keith had just picked up, Sean took a bite then turned his green gaze Susan's way and said with a confident grin, "I'm unattached because I'm smart. Truth is, I'm the only sane one in this family, hence the gorgeous green eyes."

"Due to recessive, better known as *weak,* genes," someone taunted in the background.

Rachel chuckled and continued her introductions, nodding toward Stephan talking to Jonathan. "I believe you've already met the youngest Piccoli."

Susan couldn't help but laugh and feel completely at ease with Michael's family. They each walked up and introduced themselves, always giving some amusing tidbit about each other. It was all good natured and from their comments she could tell they got along and genuinely liked one another.

"Your family likes to tease, don't they?" she whispered to Michael as handed her a plate with the cheese and crackers.

"Get used to it. Today, you're the guest and as such exempt from their torture, but the next time you're fair game," he warned with a wink.

Next time? He planned to invite her again? The thought warmed her all over. At that moment his youngest brother Stephan approached and poured himself some wine. "I've already met Susan, so does that mean *I* can tease her?"

Susan choked on her cracker and cheese as she thought about the only thing Stephan would know about her—he'd sent her to the Piccoli's wine cellar after hours with his older brother.

When she cast imploring eyes Michael's way, he chuckled

and addressed his brother. "Watch it or you'll be out of a job. Then how will you pay for all those expensive presents you buy for Alyssa?"

Stephan lifted his glass in acknowledgment. "Noted, big brother. Alyssa does have very expensive taste." A dreamy puppy dog look crossed his face before he continued, "But she's worth it."

"Speaking of Alyssa...where is your girlfriend tonight?" a petite older woman with short dark hair asked. She held her wooden cooking spoon covered with sauce out of the way and kissed Stephan on the cheek.

Stephan grimaced. "She had to study. She said to tell you she hated missing our monthly dinner and she'd be here next time, Mom."

"Good." Turning her doe brown eyes toward Susan, she came around the island and smiled as she held out her hand. "Welcome to our home, Susan. I hope you're hungry. We have five courses planned for the evening."

Five courses? Then again, I should've known Michael learned his talent for providing a great meal from his mother. Susan smiled and shook the woman's fine-boned hand. "Thank you for inviting me, Mrs. Piccoli."

She gave Susan a warm smile and squeezed her fingers. "Call me Sophia, dear. I'm glad you came tonight."

CR

Dinner at the Piccolis' was a very interactive, fun affair with much laughter and just as much ribbing. Funny, embarrassing stories were told over mouthwatering homemade pasta, gourmet salad, fluffy breadsticks and lots of wine. No one was left out of the mix. From Michael's parents to the youngest Piccoli, everyone was included in the conversations. His family even asked her to relate stories of her life with Jason and she felt so at ease, she quickly told a few amusing tales of her own.

While they were finishing up their coffee and rich mocha cheesecake for dessert, the Piccoli siblings got into a disagreement about the board game they were going to play.

"Anyone up for Monopoly? What about Scrabble? Or that new game Outburst?"

Board games...now I know why they're so important to Michael. They bring his family together at least once a month.

Finally, Michael raised his hands and said over the loud voices, "Since I'm the oldest, I'll pick. Trivial Pursuit. We'll play in teams."

While his brothers and their significant others cleared off the table and his parents retired to the living room during their game, Michael lifted Susan's hand from the table and kissed her palm. "What'd you think of dinner with the Piccolis?"

Susan smiled and answered honestly. "I can see why your restaurant is so successful. You've created an ambiance that brings people together in a wonderful, relaxing environment—a place conducive to great conversation, enjoyment of fine wines and excellent food."

Lifting her coffee cup, she said, "Imagine this is champagne as I salute your success."

Michael picked up his coffee cup and clinked it with hers. "I'm happy to share this with you, Susanna."

She was a bit surprised by his serious expression, but didn't have time to ponder it, because Michael's brothers and the women all filed into the room.

Jonathan laid the board game on the table and removed

the lid, his tone dead serious. "I'm setting the ground rules. No cheating. Got it, Joshua?" he said, his dark gaze drilling into his younger brother's.

Joshua tucked his shoulder-length black hair behind his ears and shrugged his thin shoulders. "I don't cheat."

To which everyone in the room, even his live-in girlfriend, snorted in unison. Susan raised her eyebrow in amusement. Apparently, he did.

Jonathan lifted the plastic bag that held all the game pieces and dumped the colorful wheels and wedges on the table. "Teams, pick your playing pieces."

"Grab my favorite color," Michael said to Susan while he moved his coffee cup onto the china buffet behind him.

Susan stared at all the pieces and realized everyone was waiting for her to take one before they picked theirs. *What* was *Michael's favorite color?* Feeling at a loss, she thought about how Michael had decorated his house in shades of navy blue, deep reds and taupe. Navy blue was the closest color to the pieces in front of her.

She started to pick the light blue piece when Stephan made a tsking sound and handed her the green piece instead.

As everyone else picked up their playing piece, she looked sideways at Michael. "You like green? But your house is decorated in navy blues and reds."

He nodded. "Green is my favorite color. It's just not the easiest color to decorate one's house with."

"Bet she doesn't know your favorite teddy bear growing up was named Piggy either," Stephan teased.

Susan laughed. "A teddy named Piggy?"

Michael shrugged, unapologetic. "I wanted a pet pig."

"Or that when you were a teenager you pulled off all of your braces with a set of pliers after the orthodontist said you had to wear them for another year," Sean piped in, his eyes full of laughter.

Susan winced. "Pliers?"

"See, perfectly straight." Michael flashed her a wide toothy grin.

"What about the fact—"

"That I can still torture every *single* one of my younger brothers," Michael cut Keith off, staring meaningfully around the table at each of his siblings.

"Michael's got that look." Stephan snickered. "Better save it for next time, guys."

"Okay, everyone," Jonathan said, pushing his fashionable, rimless glasses up his nose. "Let's get started so I can annihilate you all."

"And I thought *you* were competitive," Susan whispered to Michael.

He gave a low chuckle and responded in her ear. "Jonathan is the brainy one in the family. He takes this particular game very seriously."

CR

When the competitive game was over and Michael and Susan were declared the winners, Jonathan's wife, Sherri, smiled at Susan as they all filed out of the dining room. "Jon's going to go home and lick his wounds while bemoaning the fact Michael brought a 'ringer' to the table."

Susan laughed and cast an apologetic gaze Jonathan's way, but Michael's younger brother was saying goodnight to his parents by the front door. "Tell him, I'm sorry," she whispered to Sherri.

"I'm not!" Sherri's auburn eyebrows rose. "You won fair and square. He needs to stew on that for a bit."

As everyone pulled on their coats and said their goodbyes to Michael's parents, Michael whispered in Susan's ear, "I knew with you on my side, we'd kick Jonathan's butt."

"I retract my earlier comment. *You* are more competitive," she shot back with a low chuckle. "I think your brother was truly bothered he didn't win."

"Of course he was. He has never lost that game. Ever."

Once all their other children had left for their respective homes, Michael's parents turned to Michael and Susan in the foyer. "Thank you for a wonderful dinner, David and Sophia," Susan said.

"You're welcome here anytime," David said with a genuine smile before he addressed his son. "I need to ask you a question about a wine I just purchased. I don't believe your restaurant has this one and I found it quite good. Do you have a minute?"

As Michael followed his dad down the hall and through a door on the right, Sophia grasped Susan's hand. "You were a pleasure, Susanna. You fit right in with the Piccolis. I hope you'll come again."

Susan's heart swelled that Michael's mother seemed to like her. "Thank you, Sophia. I'd love to come back."

His mother gave her a knowing smile and patted Susan's arm. "You're good for Michael."

Sophia's casual comment shocked Susan. "I am?"

His mother laughed, her brown eyes sparkling. "Michael must've figured you could handle this rowdy bunch. I know they all liked you."

Swallowing the emotional lump in her throat, Susan

laughed. "It was probably because he needed a partner to help him beat his younger brother tonight." She bit her lip and continued, "I hope Jonathan isn't too upset."

Sophia squeezed her arm. "Don't you worry about Jonathan. He needed to be taken down a peg or two. He never lets anyone live it down when *he* wins."

Laughing, Susan said, "Thank you for being such a wonderful hostess, Sophia. Your family made me feel right at home."

"Of course we did. We're Piccolis," Michael announced with a wink as he entered the foyer once more.

His mother reached up and hugged her son, then kissed him on the cheek. "Take care of Susanna. She's a keeper."

Michael's gaze met Susan's over his mother's head. "I couldn't agree more."

ɒʀ

Susan and Michael stood in the lobby of her apartment complex, staring at the brushed silver elevator doors. The lobby was unusually quiet for nine o'clock on a Friday evening. Then she remembered. There was a game tonight.

Michael had taken her to a fancy restaurant and then he'd brought her back here. She was so confused, her insides felt like a metal coil tightened to its breaking point. Ever since the night she'd spent with Michael at his family's home he'd acted different toward her. He'd still been his attentive, attractive, stimulating conversationalist self, but for five nights in a row the man had left her standing at her apartment door, dumbfounded and hungering for more. Other than a quick kiss, he hadn't touched her, which was driving her sanity right to the edge.

Over the past month and a half, she'd learned to crave his hard body pressed against hers, to smell his unique masculine scent all over her skin while he made her scream in sheer fulfillment.

Every night.

With Michael's platonic behavior this week, she'd begun to wonder if she'd committed some kind of grievous error at his parents' home she was unaware of, but then at dinner tonight Michael had given her the most beautiful gift. One doesn't normally give presents to someone if they're mad or upset with them.

She glanced down at the intricate fairy charm that hung from the delicate gold chain around her neck.

With its back arched and its wings tucked, the fairy smiled skyward, appearing to be enjoying the wind in its waist-length hair. The way the fairy hung on the necklace, its pixie face stared directly at her.

"So your parents can continue to watch over you, no matter where you are," Michael had said when she'd opened the jewelry box.

She'd cried over his incredibly thoughtful gift.

Hence her current confused state.

As the elevator doors slid open, she realized excitement would be growing in her belly right about now...if she hadn't had the last five frustrating evenings to stew on. Tonight they were alone in the elevator. Once the heavy doors slowly slid closed and the elevator began to move upward, a sudden, jolting thought occurred...one she hadn't considered until this very moment, driving her self-esteem into the ground.

Hard.

Had he lost interest? Was he was trying to figure out a way to stop seeing her and the fairy necklace was a parting gift? The thought slammed her in the gut, making her almost double over as her body experienced true, physical pain.

She forced her shoulders to straighten and took a deep breath. Casting her gaze Michael's way, she hoped he hadn't noticed.

He looked mouthwatering and devastating in his custom-made business suit. His white shirt and deep red tie made his olive skin seem even darker. Droplets of rain glistened across his broad shoulders, highlighting his strong jawline, reflecting in his pitch black hair like tiny diamonds. Her fingers itched to slide through the thick, silky locks and rub away the moisture.

Her gaze drifted to his handsome hands and she was surprised to discover they were curled inward instead of hanging relaxed by his sides.

This...this distance he'd put between them bewildered her, but she didn't know how to broach the subject without looking like a clingy, needy woman.

Until an idea came to her.

She'd make him want to stay tonight.

Rubbing her suddenly damp palms across her black skirt, Susan reached out and pulled the red emergency button, thankful no blaring alarms went off in the process.

When the unit came to an abrupt halt, Michael's eyebrow rose and he looked at her.

Susan inhaled to calm her nerves and turned to walk right into Michael's personal space. "Remember when we talked about having sex in a public place?" she asked as she unbuttoned his jacket.

When she began to tug on his tie, his warm hands

encircled her wrists, stopping her movements. "No, we didn't. You asked if I'd ever had sex in public." His chocolate brown gaze searched hers and his hands tightened around her wrists. "And I said, 'yes'."

Her breath caught at the look of banked desire reflected in his gaze. Hope rose within her. She splayed her hands across his hard chest then slid her nails over his nipples. Dropping her gaze to his chest, she said, "How many times have we ridden this elevator up to my apartment?"

"At least forty," he responded, his thumbs rubbing small circles along the soft insides of her wrists.

"And how many times have you wanted to have your way with me against one of these walls?"

"All forty."

Her heart skipped several beats at the unadulterated intensity in his tone. No hesitation, just blunt honesty.

But it was the sensation of his erection brushing against her lower belly, combined with the hunger in his eyes, that snatched the breath right out of her lungs.

Tugging her wrists from his hold, she ran her fingers slowly down his cock and wrapped them around the hard outline in a firm grip. With an intentional challenge lacing her tone, she said, "Then what's stopping you—"

The words weren't even out of her mouth before his hands cupped her face and his mouth claimed hers in a dominant, possessive kiss.

Yes! She mentally rejoiced as Michael slanted his mouth over hers, thrusting his tongue deep. She kissed him back with just as much passion, tangling her tongue with his.

Somewhere deep within him, she felt a rumbling growl in his chest. He crowded her, walking her backward a couple of steps until her back pressed against the cool elevator wall.

He took no prisoners, his tongue exploring every dip and hollow in her mouth at the same time he shoved his thigh between hers. His hands, both rough and warm, began to slide her skirt up, exposing her thighs.

Susan dug her nails into his shoulders, the rich material crushing under her fingers as her heart rate skyrocketed. She'd never seen him like this, aggressive and edgy, on the verge of losing total control.

Damn, she loved it!

She broke their kiss and whispered in his ear, "Don't stop. I love your hands on me, touching me everywhere. When you look at me, you make me melt. I feel like the most cherished woman in the world when I'm with you—special and unique in every way."

"The way you smell, the way you move...you drive me out of my fucking mind," he said in a hoarse, tortured, husky tone as he skimmed his lips across her jaw.

Susan thrilled when he moved his cock between her thighs and his hands grasped her buttocks through her silky underwear, lifting her off the ground slightly so he could grind against her. Her core throbbed and her breasts ached for his touch—her entire body shook with need to feel him deep inside her.

"Then we're even, considering the way you've left me wanting this week," she replied when his lips pressed against her throat.

Michael froze, every part of his body stilled and tensed at once.

The moment he began to pull away, a part of her soul went with him. Susan gripped his shoulders, her stomach churning. "What's wrong? Why'd you stop?"

Michael growled and turned away from her, slamming his hands through his hair.

Susan felt like someone was stomping on her chest, twisting the toe of their shoe in delighted glee as she slowly tried to breathe. Fear that she was losing him made defensive anger surface. "What did I do wrong? What do you want from me?"

He whirled on her, his hands dropping to fists by his sides as he snarled, "I want you to give a damn, Susanna!"

Chapter Nine

He wanted her to give a damn?

Astonishment ricocheted through her, knocking her in the gut. That was the last thing she'd expected to hear from him. "What are you talking about, of course I give a—"

"No, you don't," he cut her off, his tone angrier than she'd ever heard it.

Stepping into her personal space, he continued, his expression fierce, "Sex between us is...damn...I can't even put a word to it, it's that good, yet I know there's more between us. Only you won't let me mean more to you."

Susan's safe world, the one she'd created to keep her heart intact, was crumbling around her. "What are you talking about? You mean a lot to me."

"Do I?" he challenged, his expression doubtful. "I know you grew up feeling like a gawky kid, that your favorite color is purple, that jazz music relaxes you while pop turns you on, that you talk and make sexy little sounds in your sleep, that your favorite toy as a kid was a Raggedy Ann doll, that you miss your parents a great deal and if one more person asks you to be in yet another wedding as their maid of honor, you'll commit hari-kari."

Michael shocked the hell out of her with his diatribe. She had no idea he'd paid so much attention. Then again, he'd given her a fairy necklace to "watch over her", which meant he'd remembered her story about "why" she continued to collect fairies. Finally she realized what was bothering him. She touched his cheek and her gaze searched his. "I know that you're the oldest of five boys, that you love a good merlot, that you're a very talented cook, that you'll go out of your way to repay old debts—"

"All things I've told you about myself, Susanna." His hand covered hers, hurt reflected in his gaze. "I want you to *want* to know everything about me. To care enough to ask."

His last comment floored her, making her stomach lurch as if the elevator had dropped three floors. She had no idea Michael felt so strongly. When she thought back to when he'd begun to distance himself from her sexually, it had all started right after they'd had dinner with his family. During the game, she hadn't known his favorite color or anything about his childhood. In reality, she hadn't asked him direct, intimate questions about himself or his past because she didn't want to get too emotionally close to him. But the truth was, she had soaked up all there was about Michael on her own, despite her best efforts to remain at an emotional distance.

Grasping his hand, she smiled. "I know you like toast with marmalade for breakfast, but you'll toss the whole thing if the bread's not crisp enough for you, that you forget to put the cap on your toothpaste, not because you're lazy, but because you set the cap you've rinsed down to dry and forget to put it back on, that your favorite music is soft jazz, that you read the newspaper from back to front, that your family means more to you than you'll ever admit to them, that you love the fact you're the oldest of your siblings and by the nature of being so, always the one to take charge."

At the look of complete surprise on his face, she tilted her head to the side and grinned. "Does that about sum you up in a

213

nutshell, Michael Piccoli?"

"How do you know all that?" He turned her hand over and kissed her palm, his expression shifting to amazement.

"Because I cared enough to pay attention."

In spite of all her efforts to keep him at an emotional arm's-length, she realized just how much she'd fallen in love with the handsome Italian. One day she'd tell him how she felt. For now, she linked her fingers with his, just content to share a special moment with him.

When his expression turned serious, she asked, "What is it?"

Michael shook his dark head and flashed a brief smile. "Nothing. I just like looking at you." As he ran his thumb along her jaw, his gaze searched her face. "I've lived long enough to know what I want in my life and I definitely want you in it."

His comment warmed her all over. Susan closed her eyes and leaned her cheek against his palm. "I love having you in my life, too."

"Susanna, I'm asking you to marry me."

Her gaze jerked to his, eyes wide in surprise. "Marry you?"

He palmed her cheeks with his warm hands. "I know you think this is sudden and I'm willing to wait a year if you wish for a longer engagement, but I know I want you. I knew the moment I touched your hand that first day at my restaurant. *We* were meant to be."

"I..." She was so shocked, she was speechless...both thrilled and frightened. A sinking sensation began to spread in her stomach. Marriage? The thought of giving Michael that kind of power to possibly hurt her made her chest ache.

His gaze locked with hers. "I love you very much."

Her skin prickled at his declaration. "Michael...I—"

"What's wrong, Susanna?" His brow furrowed. "I know you care for me, but you've held back a part of yourself ever since the day we met. I've felt it and had hoped over time you'd come to trust me, especially after meeting my family."

"I thought you brought me there to kick your brother's butt and because you knew I liked board games."

He frowned at her. "Couldn't you see what I was doing? I wanted you to meet my family because you were important to me. I've never taken another woman to my parents' house."

She had no idea that she'd been the only one. "I—I thought since Stephan brings his girlfriend each month that was why you felt comfortable inviting me—that friends were included in the Piccoli family circle."

He shook his head, his gaze intense. "Stephan falls in and out of love about as often as he changes his clothes. That's not who I am."

Michael had been completely honest with her. He deserved the truth. Susan swallowed the lump in her throat. "Every person who has meant something to me has moved on...my parents, my uncle...and recently my brother. I just didn't want to open myself up to the possibility of that kind of emptiness yet again." Her gaze dropped to his tie as she finished, "Marriage...well, it scares me."

He tilted her chin up with his finger. Understanding reflected in his eyes, his gaze steady and tender. "Have you considered the fact I've opened myself up to be hurt as well? I told you I loved you and have asked you to marry me without knowing for sure how you truly feel about me...about us. Loving another person is a risk worth taking."

Michael *had* taken a big chance emotionally with her. The man rocked her world. He was the kind of man she thought she'd never meet, the kind of man she completely respected...the man she knew she loved. She thought of how happy she was in the dream she'd had about Michael and her. And the real-life Michael had turned out to be exactly like the Michael in her dream—a loving, generous man who wanted to share his life with her in every respect.

For the first time in her life, she decided to follow her emotions and her heart. Refusing to allow herself second thoughts or doubts, she jumped into his arms and wrapped her legs around his waist.

Kissing him square on the mouth, she said with a laugh, "How's this for an answer?"

Michael started to speak when a voice came through on the loud speaker, interrupting them. Rounds of applause and catcalls sounded in the background. "If the show's over, do you think you could press the red button back in? We've got a crowd down here waiting to use the elevator."

Mortified heat flooded Susan's cheeks and she glanced around the elevator for signs of a camera.

"To your right and up a little. See the decorative glass ball in the corner?" the disembodied voice came through the speakers again.

Her gaze jerked to the corner he described and Susan's stomach pitched. A hidden camera must be behind the ball. She had no idea.

"There ya go. Wave to the crowd of voyeurs behind me. Think you can hit that button now?"

Gripping one of Michael's shoulders tight, Susan leaned over and pushed the button. As the elevator began to move, she lowered her feet to the floor and glanced down to make sure her disheveled clothes covered everything. Suddenly, a sneaking suspicion wormed its way into her mind. Michael was being way too quiet.

She narrowed her gaze on him. "You knew, didn't you?" she mumbled.

He gave a low chuckle. "I suspected."

Despite her embarrassment, Susan laughed. She couldn't help it. He always made her smile.

Michael's laugher slowed and he gently squeezed her waist. "As much as I love your enthusiasm, I'd kind of like to hear the words."

"Me, too," someone grumbled in a grouchy tone.

Michael grinned at Ms. Jenkins' scowl. Neither one of them had noticed that the elevator had stopped at Susan's floor and the doors had opened. He scooped Susan up and walked off the elevator, saying to the older lady as she got on the elevator, "It's our fortieth date and she's about to say yes."

"I'll just bet she is," Ms. Jenkins snapped in disdain right before the doors closed behind her.

As Michael carried her down the hall, Susan didn't care that in her current position with her legs wrapped around his waist her short dress probably showed her underwear. At least she was wearing some! She was too happy to worry about appearances. And at this point, her entire apartment building knew she had the hots for the tall, dark-haired man. When Michael set her feet on the floor next to her door, she kept her arms wrapped around his shoulders and smiled up at him as he smoothed down her skirt.

"I love you, Michael Piccoli. I love everything about your sexy Italian self. From your strong work ethic, to your self-confidence, to your tenacity in business as well as your dedication to family and friends. I think I'll like being the woman you love."

"Does that mean yes?" he asked, linking his hands at the base of her spine to pull her close.

"There's that tenacity." She laughed, nodding. "It most definitely means yes. We can discuss the long engagement part later," she finished with a wink.

When Michael's shoulders began to shake in suppressed laughter, she eyed him warily. "What's so amusing?"

He gave her a naughty grin, the one that always made her melt.

"I can't wait to see the look on Melanie's face when you ask her to be your *matron* of honor."

Susan laughed so hard tears filled her eyes. Pulling him close, she didn't care that they were standing in the hall for anyone to see. Instead, she brushed her lips against his and whispered, "I love how you bring out this spontaneous, emotional side in me."

"It was always there, Susanna..." Michael paused and trailed kisses across her cheek until his lips hovered over hers "...waiting to be seduced out of you."

Susan tilted her head toward her apartment and said in a sexy tone, "Speaking of seducing me...you have some lost time to make up for, mister. And don't think I'm not going to make you pay."

"Promise?" Michael whispered in a husky voice while she slid her key in the lock.

God, the man just makes me melt, she thought as she opened the door.

Once Michael followed her inside and pushed the door closed behind him, she arched her eyebrow and stepped back, her pulse already thumping. "Does your 'promise' question go back to our very first date where you said you'd being willing to give up control with the right incentive?"

Michael shrugged out of his jacket and tossed it on the

chair next to the couch. After he pulled off his tie, he let it dangle suggestively in his hand, then advanced on her. Unbuttoning his shirt with his other hand, he swept his seductive gaze over her body in blatant lust. "In answer to your query, my question was *entirely* related to my statement about giving up control."

Susan's body heat rose at his predatory approach. There was nothing acquiescent or submissive about it. Before she could say a word, he quickly grabbed her around the waist and tossed her over his shoulder.

"Michael!" She smacked him on the butt. "This doesn't look like you're giving up control to me."

"Oh, I'm more than willing, sweetheart. You'll just have to figure out what that incentive is," he said in a wicked tone as he carried her off to the bedroom.

About the Author

Born and raised in the Southeast, award-winning author Patrice Michelle gave up her financial calculator for a keyboard and never looked back. Thanks to an open-minded family who taught her that life isn't as black and white as we're conditioned to believe, she pens her novels with the belief that various shades of gray are a lot more interesting. She's a natural with a point-and-shoot camera, likes to fiddle with graphic design and, to the relief of her family, strums her guitar to an audience of one.

Patrice also writes sexy, heart-tugging contemporary and paranormal romances and dark, seductive paranormal romances.

You can visit Patrice to learn more about her novels, read excerpts, join her yahoo group and sign up for her newsletter at www.patricemichelle.net.

*Psychic matchmaker Cally gives everyone their happy ending.
But can she ever have one herself?*

Touch Me
© *2007 Beverly Rae*

When Sloan Janson's best friend makes a sudden marriage after being "matched" by Cally, Sloan is convinced his friend is the victim of a con. He storms into Cally's small Texas town, determined to expose her as a fraud. The minute he meets her, he still wants to expose her, but now in a totally different sense!

Years of matching soul mates, however satisfying, hasn't prepared Cally for the electrical effect Sloan has on her. She's tempted, and terrified—she's always known matchmakers can't have love without blowing the fuse on their gift.

Her worst fears come true when her ability to match deserts her. If she cuts Sloan out of her life, she's sure it will return. But is that a choice she can bear to make—or to live with?

Available now in ebook and print from Samhain Publishing.

*The sheriff has the hots for her prime suspect.
What's a girl to do?*

Too Good to be True
© 2007 Marie-Nicole Ryan

Sheriff Rilla Devane has sworn to serve and protect, just as her father did before he was murdered. An influx of party drugs has killed two teenagers, but she has a suspect: handsome, rich newcomer Mackenzie Callahan, a published author seeking small-town atmosphere. To build her case, she moves closer to Mackenzie and his dangerous brand of seductive charm. She'll risk everything for her investigation, even when it means letting her guard down and falling for her suspect.

Mac Callahan lives and breathes for undercover work. But his last mission ended in near disaster, and he has one last chance to prove his value to the DEA. Taking sexy Sheriff Rilla to bed might ruin his career—or lead him to the love of his life.

Available now in ebook and print from Samhain Publishing.

hot stuff

Discover Samhain!

THE HOTTEST NEW PUBLISHER ON THE PLANET

Romance, fantasy, mystery, thriller, mainstream and
more—Samhain has more selection, hotter authors, and
everything's available in both ebook and print.

Pick your favorite, sit back, and enjoy the ride!
Hot stuff indeed.

Samhain
Publishing
ltd

WWW.SAMHAINPUBLISHING.COM

GREAT CHEAP FUN

Discover eBooks!

THE FASTEST WAY TO GET THE HOTTEST NAMES

Get your favorite authors on your favorite reader, long before they're
out in print! Ebooks from Samhain go wherever you go, and work with
whatever you carry—Palm, PDF, Mobi, and more.

Printed in the United States
204516BV00002B/1-129/P